A Dash of Daring

A Spirited Spinters Sweet Regency Romance

ROBYN CHALMERS

Cover Art by Carpe Librum Book Design

Edited by Voirey Linger & Lia Fairchild

Proofing by Debbie Phillips at DP+

~

JOIN MY READERS GROUP
https://www.robynchalmers.com/newsletter

For TJ

I remember the day I looked into your eyes and saw my future.
And then we made it together.
Thank you.

CHAPTER 1

IN WHICH AN EARL IS FOUND IN THE STABLE
WITH A SHOVEL, SUFFOLK COUNTY, JULY 1808

Diana Kingsley strode across the garden, in full view of her new stepmother's drawing room window, an apple in each pocket of her riding habit.

It was high time the new Mrs. Kingsley learned Diana was six-and-twenty and did not need to be schooled on manners, deportment, or any other ladylike accomplishments she felt were lacking.

The thought of being cooped up in that drawing room made her skin itch. Head down, she lengthened her stride, each step taking her closer to the stables and freedom. Today, with its warm breeze and clear blue sky, was not a day to sit inside and practice one's needlework.

If she could just saddle Equinox quickly enough, an entire morning of trousseau preparations would be avoided. How many embroidered handkerchiefs did a newly married lady need in any case?

With every step she was further from her stepmother's deceptively calm voice calling her back. "Diana, if I could have a word?" She let out a sigh of relief as she arrived at the training quadrangle.

The Kingsley stables were still new enough to be of constant delight, a compound of beautiful sandstone buildings that were the latest and best in equestrian management.

Diana stopped short and frowned when she saw Equinox in the training ring by Ned. Her beautiful boy had long since retired from racing and was well and truly at stud. He had nothing to prove to anyone, no reason to be put through his paces.

Her father, famous thoroughbred breeder Beau Kingsley, leaned on the fence as she'd seen him do a thousand times before. Dressed in his usual tailored navy superfine, with buckskin breeches and a crisp white cravat, Father looked more aristocratic than his guest, who wore an ill-cut coat of drab brown. She did not recognize him.

The sun warmed her back, and the breeze pulled hair from her loose bun into her face. Diana brushed them aside and squinted, trying to place the man Father was with. His stiff back spoke of the army, while his softly padded frame suggested a man who hadn't used his body in battle for some time.

Seeing army men at the Kingsley stables was not unusual because many of the regiments purchased horses from their stables. It broke her heart every time, and she wished her Father wouldn't sell them into such a grim life.

But at least this man would not be looking at Equinox for that reason; he was far too valuable at stud.

As if in answer, Equinox threw his head back and neighed loudly, shaking his mane. He always put on a show, like he was the most headstrong horse imaginable. For her, with an apple and a few sweet words, he was ready for any adventure.

"He's magnificent," she heard the man say as the wind carried their voices toward her. "So much fire…"

The men stayed silent for a few moments, admiring Equinox as he pranced around the ring.

Her father spotted her and beckoned her over. She smoothed her hair and went to his side.

"Diana, may I introduce you to Major Bloomfield. He acts as aide to the Prince of Wales."

The prince! Diana bobbed a curtsey, her mind racing. Nobody from anywhere as illustrious as the royal stables had visited the Kingsley Estate for years.

Not since she had ruined herself.

The ton had stayed away in droves, choosing Father's competitors to buy their horses from.

That's what happened when you jilted an earl of the realm so publicly, whether he deserved it or not. Especially when your family was not on the same social strata. The Kingsleys were definitely gentry, holding substantial land to breed their horses. But they weren't titled; nobody in the family was.

Perhaps all had been forgiven, now that she was finally engaged again. This time to a duke's nephew. No title, but still a connection that reestablished the Kingsleys as "good ton."

"I'm pleased to make your acquaintance." *So pleased someone so illustrious has arrived, so I can let go of some of the guilt I've been carrying around like a tattered reticule all these years.*

He took in her riding attire, a smile tugging at his lips. "Going out for a gallop then? Lovely morning for it!"

"If you must know, I have escaped my stepmother's rigorous embroidery schedule." She put her finger to her lips. "Shhh."

Diana took her leave. But she stayed close. Then, after a few minutes, Father shook the man's hand with a hearty laugh and waved him off. Returning to the stable, he stopped short when he saw her, his cheeks flooding with color. "You may have guessed what is happening."

"The prince wants to use Equinox as a stud horse?" Before long half of England's racehorses would be sired by him. Not really, but the thought made her smile.

Father shook his head. "Close. The prince wants to purchase him."

"A dream doomed to be crushed," she said, holding out both

hands for her father to take. He did not take them and her stomach fell. "Oh no, please say you didn't."

If a horse could be the jewel in the crown of the Kingsley stables, Equinox was a fist-sized unflawed diamond. He had finished his five-year racing career with twenty-one wins, including twelve King's Plates. More than any horse in England, Ireland, Scotland, or Wales. He was the stuff of legends.

He was *her* legend. He raced for her, she knew it. Something tightened in her chest, and suddenly it was hard to breathe. Because more than that, he was her best friend. She had assumed he would comprise part of her dowry once more, and live with her forever. It was hardly his fault that this marriage was a means to an end.

Father shrugged in a way that suggested the bargain was sealed. "I must. The prince is opening his new royal stables in Brighton in three weeks and wants Equinox there. If the prince is buying from us, everyone will deal with us once again. There can be no greater endorsement."

She shook her head. "Then give him some yearlings, for pity's sake. Not the best horse we have."

"That would not be quite the spectacle that Equinox is. And, the prince has invited us to the opening of the stables. Not an opportunity I have any intention of missing. Cordelia is most excited."

Pulling on his hand and begging him would be a mistake, but something must be said. "Think, Father, just last year he sold off his *entire* stud to pay his debts. How can you trust him not to do the same again?" The outrage wanted to burst forth in a horrible river of tears, but that never helped matters and allowed him to label her "hysterical." So, she tamped it down and took a deep, shaky breath.

"I'm sure he has learned his lesson well. Equinox will live out his days in royal stables."

Diana swept her arm to take in the entire stable area. "More like he must leave his only home, and all the people he loves, so we can reestablish our good name. I thought my engagement might have done that for us."

His lips were compressed, with a white edge around them. "Every little bit helps."

She drew in a shocked breath. "I hardly think agreeing to marry a man fifteen years my senior, nor you selling our best horse, are little things." One alone felt earth-shattering, two was more than her mind could comprehend.

His jaw was set, and he looked at her steadily. "No, although you must admit your situation *was* of your own making."

It was cruel to remind her of that time, now five years past; it was best put in a dark little box, tied with string, placed in the topmost shelf in the attic, pushed to the back and covered with a blanket. But social annihilation just didn't die that easily. Luckily, neither did her conviction that she had done the right thing.

"I regret nothing. My life would have been intolerable with Lord Fortescue. I remain happy to do my duty and marry Colonel Webster, who gives me no such qualms. But why should Equinox suffer?"

He crossed his arms, his mouth pursed in annoyance. "I hardly think being the prince's prize horse will be a hardship."

Diana looked down at her boot and traced a pattern in the dust, ignoring *that* statement. "Was it Mrs. Kingsley's idea to take Equinox out of my dowry and use him thus?" At this point she couldn't bring herself to call her either Cordelia or Stepmother.

His eyes narrowed. "Sometimes I wish you were not so quick, Diana."

"Sometimes I wish it too." Surely, she would feel things less keenly. His betrayal was making her hands shake. "Just once, I wish you would choose me and my needs over what is best for Kingsley Stud. Seeing your priorities so baldly continues to hurt."

His eyes focused on her trembling hands for a moment too long. Then he looked away, and nothing had ever felt so cold.

"Hurtful or not, Mrs. Kingsley reminded me that *last* time Equinox formed part of your dowry, we did not attract the *right* kind of suitor."

He was not wrong. And she'd found out almost too late that such was the case. It was hard to learn he was not actually her horse this way, though. "What did the prince pay?"

He sighed, conveying his annoyance at having to talk about something as commonplace as money with her. "Two thousand guineas, if you must know. The highest amount ever paid for a racehorse."

She gasped, her hand flying to her mouth involuntarily. A small fortune. Any thought she had for buying him back with her meagre savings faded. "Have you signed a contract?"

"Not yet. It will come in the next week."

Her hands trembled again, so she clutched them together. Father saw that too. "There is nothing you can do. I have shaken hands with the man. The prince will get the king of horses. It is fitting, in a way. Equinox will be the star of the stable opening. And, I hasten to tell you, I have made one stipulation: Honey has to go with him, or there's no deal."

Relief rushed over the anxiety. "Oh, thank goodness! At least he will not be entirely alone." It didn't make it better, but it helped. The pony was like a warm blanket for her seventeen-hand stallion; they always grazed in the same field and were often found resting together under a tree.

"I let him know Equinox becomes completely unruly and impossible to control without Honey." He smiled sadly. "But he already knew. Honey's fame precedes her."

It was much the same way Diana was known by all and sundry as Lady Luck because Equinox won whenever she attended the races. The times she had not attended, he had not even placed. It happened often enough that punters would look for her in the crowd before placing their bets.

"I'm still not happy." But they were in the business of breeding and selling horses. She should know better than to become so hopelessly attached to him. "I will do whatever I can to get him back to us after the prince's precious stable opening." It was the only thought that made it bearable. Her mind was already racing through an inventory of what she could sell to raise funds. But two thousand guineas. It was impossible.

"I would expect no less. Although I do hope you'll stop short of outright theft." He waggled a finger at her, trying to lighten the mood. "You will just have to trust me on this. I know it may seem hasty, but I have not built these stables without meticulous planning and attention to detail. The contract will have clauses ensuring we can send mares to him to sire more foals. We just won't have him wandering in the fields all day. Promise me you won't do anything foolish."

He had good reason to ask the question.

Diana shook her head. "I promise nothing. I care little about the foals, but a great deal about him being in my fields every day."

He smiled and put an arm around her. "Incorrigible. Will you come back to the house with me?"

She shrugged herself out of his embrace and walked toward the stall where Equinox was now waiting for her. "No, I will take my dear boy for as many rides as he will let me, for as long as we have him."

Once there, she pulled an apple from her pocket. "Did they make you show off then, did they? And no apple afterward?"

He took the fruit from her and crunched happily, then pushed his nose into her hand for another. His warm brown eyes met hers as though in understanding. She hugged his neck. There was no way the wastrel prince was going to keep him. She'd move heaven and earth to make sure this relocation was of the shortest possible term.

She was lost in thought, mindlessly stroking his neck, when somebody called her name.

"Ahoy there, Miss Kingsley." She looked up. Alec, Lord Templeton, stood in the opposite stall.

She looked around the stalls for her brother—because where Templeton was, Pip invariably followed—but she couldn't see him.

He was dressed in working breeches and a white shirt, with no cravat in sight. In other words, it was Lord Templeton stripped of his usual sartorial glory and looking like a stable hand. A small triangle of tan skin at his throat demanded her attention and she had to force herself to look away.

Even clothed in crumpled clothes, he was beautiful. Like a dark-haired pirate, all lithe and sprung with energy, ready to bound over the decks with sword in hand.

Just looking at him made her long for … for *something*. Adventure, perhaps? When she was younger, just having him in the same room made her to light up like a hundred-candle chandelier.

Even his lack of any kind of offer over ten whole years had done nothing to dull his effect on her. It was exhausting, because as long as he remained unattached, her heart refused to give up all hope.

But now with another man's betrothal ring on her hand, the hopes and dreams of her youth could not be allowed to hold her back from her future.

The boy next door simply did not love her back.

Her stomach lurched, as though memories of that hope were only yesterday. Waiting for him to court her when she made her debut. Having *three* dances with him at her coming-out ball. Being led into supper and him bringing her a plate of nibbles and her first glass of champagne. Thinking from their lively flirting that he finally saw her as more than an annoying little sister to be rescued from scrapes.

Engaging herself to Lord Fortescue when that never happened.

Waiting for him to realize that after his father died, she would help him through.

Just waiting.

Then realizing he would never wake up, no matter how often she flirted with him as though her life depended on it.

The usual irritation rose. *Damn you, Templeton. No wonder I love Equinox. He actually loves me back.*

He leaned on a shovel and watched her with his usual lazy gaze. His eyes looked almost black in the dull stable light. But in proper daylight they were the color of dark rum.

"In the doldrums, Miss Kingsley?" He motioned to Equinox. "Perhaps you should take him for a ride. Nothing like the wind in one's hair to raise the spirits."

All she needed a moment to take a breath and settle herself after the shock of Equinox being sold. But Templeton was the last person to calm her roaring emotions. Quite the opposite.

Diana fixed him with a stony stare, eyebrows raised. "My dear Lord Templeton, how lovely to see you. Although you were at last night's assembly, were you not?" She had found over the years that the best defense against his charm was a brutal offense.

His brown eyes lit, acknowledging her deflection. "Indeed, I was. Were you there too? I'm sorry we did not dance, if you were."

She shook her head slowly in disbelief, because their eyes had locked more than once during the evening. He truly loved to spar with her, and perhaps indulging him would burn off some of the horrid swirling in her stomach that grew with each thought of losing her horse.

She took a brush hanging from the stall wall and applied it to Equinox's glossy mane. "You surprise me. I know you saw me, and one would think you'd love to dance with such an old friend. Although, I suppose I do not qualify as potential wifely material."

"Correct. Father always wanted me to save him by marrying an heiress. My reply was ever that I would rather choke and die with my face in porridge than give him the satisfaction of a wealthy bride. My bride will come from the gutter, if I have anything to say about it, and bring with her a family of twenty penniless aunts who I will install in Althorne Park in triumph."

Diana smiled, even as her heart twisted at the thought. "And cats. There must be a menagerie of cats and any other stray animals you can round up."

"Exactly!" he said, his eyes lighting. "But now that he is gone, of course, I find I cannot marry an heiress for entirely different reasons."

She shrugged one shoulder. "You are not very attractive to them, perhaps?" *Present company excluded.*

He laughed. "Well, there's that."

She pretended to think about it. "Or they're not attractive to you? All those years searching for a guttersnipe has changed you?"

He raised a single eyebrow, one of his signature expressions. "Oh, I'm not particular. Don't be misled. A good heart is my only requirement. The problem is, how can I marry for *anything* but love?"

She blinked in mock horror. "Good lord, you're a romantic. That would have been my very last guess." *You never fell in love with me.*

He raised a finger to his lips. "Please don't tell anyone. If Pip finds out, my life will not be worth living."

Lowering her voice, Diana leaned toward him, getting a healthy dose of his lemon verbena mixed with hard work scent. It was heady stuff. "Your secret is safe with me. I shall put it in my famous secret chamber."

"I have it on good authority that your secret chamber can be easily accessed with a glass of champagne or two at supper."

She lifted her chin. "Lies! Name one secret I have divulged."

"That Pip let Equinox in a field with the wrong horses, and now you have a couple of *very* closely related foals?"

"Ha! That was never in the chamber. It was much too entertaining. But none of this answers why you did not stand up with me last night." She loved to dance with him. It felt like flying.

Templeton smiled at his boots, a small secret smile that suggested he was thinking something he dare not voice. As if that ever happened. "My instinct for self-preservation informed my decision. I was not of a mind to be skewered by your conversation."

"Why ever would I skewer you, Lord Templeton? I assure you I have the utmost regard for you."

As they were growing up, Lord Templeton had spent many summer holidays at Kingsley House. Some might say he was almost like a brother. Except that was laughable. He had never felt like a brother. More like a boy demi-god who she would gladly trail after if only he'd drop her a crumb. But he seemed more inclined to just poke and tease her.

He did not behave like that with other ladies. She'd watched him at last night's assembly. He charmed every lady he stood up with, from debutantes to their mothers, and sometimes even their grandmothers. They generally finished dancing with him, slightly bewildered and patting their hair. And it wasn't just because he had a windswept poetic look to him or a jaw you could likely hew wood on—because any gentleman could be handsome. No, it was because he looked at them like whatever they were saying was important to him, like they were the only person in the room.

But none of that charm was ever aimed at her. Instead, she got the Templeton who took anything she was trying to hide and lifted it to the light like an interesting specimen he found in the mud on a riverbank.

"Oh, you'd find a way. It wouldn't be long before you were discovering that I had spilled champagne on my cravat or lost the buckle on my shoe. Then you would tease me without mercy, and then *I* would have to tease *you* in retaliation and before we knew it, the entire dance floor would be a battlefield, with you and I left bloody and bruised before the quadrille was over." He shrugged. "So, you see, I did both of us a favor by not asking you to dance last night."

He punctuated his last sentence with a jab of his shovel onto the bricked floor. "And, in any case, you were always occupied with some country squire or other. Your derriere did not touch the seat of a chair for the entire evening."

"Templeton!"

"You most certainly did not need me to dance with you, unless it was to prove that *every* gentleman in the room was under your spell."

"Oh, I should *never* think that of you. You are far too tough a nut to crack."

"And you are far too hard a toffee for me to try."

She blinked. They seemed to be talking about something entirely different, but it was impossible to tell exactly what. "Me? A toffee? We both know I am not that sweet."

"Exactly. You are one of those toffees that you can't quite decide whether it is sweet or bitter, because the cook took it too far, but then after a moment of concentration, you decide, no, it's just bitter."

"Oh! You beast!" A swift stab of hurt was followed by anger. She scowled in consternation, trying to stop the rush of tears. This morning had been more than enough. She dipped her head, and he dipped his, too, looking into her eyes when she would rather he went to Hades.

She could swear she heard him swear under his breath. "Damnation."

"I'm sorry, Diana. I went too far."

"I do not believe I have given you leave of my name." But of course, she had, back when she was ten.

"Miss Kingsley," Lord Templeton said formally. "Please

forgive my insult to your good person." He sounded like he meant it.

She waved him away, not wanting him to think, for even a moment, that she was soft. She could bear many things from him, but not his pity. "Oh, no need to apologize. I enjoy having one man on earth who treats me as an equal. Pray, continue to think of me as a bitter toffee."

She strode off, leaving him behind, all thought of her ride gone. "With any luck, you'll chip your tooth, then choke on it."

"That's my huntress," she heard him say softly behind her. "Skewered me well and good. But whatever has happened to put you out of sorts?"

CHAPTER 2

IN WHICH PASTRY THEFT SHOULD BE TAKEN
MORE SERIOUSLY

Alec seated himself at the Kingsley dinner table with a small sigh that was part exhaustion and part sheer delight at the feast that had been laid before him. Casseroles, soup, pastries, and joints of meat galore. It was almost as if they were expecting someone important, and he was quite sure it wasn't him. He hadn't eaten this well since ... well, since the last time he'd dined with the Kingsleys. Bless them.

His stomach rumbled embarrassingly.

Nobody at this table would ever look at him and think: *This lord of the realm has been eating with his servants to save money for a new solicitor.* One who was brave enough to take on a prince.

No, people did not generally look at earls and think *poverty-stricken* and especially not the Earls Templeton, who were known for their high-flying ways and ability to loan even princes of the kingdom vast sums of money.

Empire-crumbling amounts of money.

Money, unfortunately, that said princes did not think it necessary to repay. He discovered quickly that their entire existence was nothing more than a house of cards, and Father's death had blown it all down.

So, free lodging and meals for a week was most welcome, and doubly so when he had the opportunity to learn about horse breeding from England's best. Certainly, he lived close by, but the mornings were early at the stables, and it was easier just to roll downstairs than ride over each day.

Mrs. Kingsley had seated him next to Diana, since there wasn't much choice at the small family dinner. Guests tended to float in and out of the Kingsley estate, but there was nobody but immediate family tonight. They still ate in the formal dining room, he and Diana on one side, Pip and Mrs. Kingsley on the other, while Mr. Kingsley took the head of the table next to his wife. A small fire blazed in the hearth to keep the chill off the air.

The new Mrs. Kingsley, whose headpiece for dinner sported a fern with a small artificial bluebird perched on it, had a sharp-eyed look about her, as though she could sum the value of your ensemble in a swift glance. "Good evening, Lord Templeton," she said with a tight smile. "I trust you had a rewarding day?"

Alec nodded. "I must have because there is not a bone in my body that does not ache. This horse breeding business is quite demanding."

She inclined her head. "So I hear. I am always glad Mr. Kingsley has stepped back from the rigorous work and has his men take care of it."

"Or so I tell you," Mr. Kingsley replied, and they all laughed.

Had living with the new stepmother forced Diana into a hasty engagement? He lived and went to church in the same parish as the Kingsleys and hadn't heard the banns called. Because he would have been the first to stand up and stop it on any grounds necessary.

"And how is your dear mother?" Mrs. Kingsley continued.

In utter denial about our circumstances. "Very happily engrossed in an old Maria Edgeworth novel last I heard."

"Oh, I must borrow it from her when she is finished. Perhaps she would come to dinner?" Mrs. Kingsley was forever angling to have the Dowager Countess of Templeton visit. But Mother had retreated into her own world since Father died, and rarely paid visits.

Alec smiled to take the sting from the rejection he was about to serve her. "You will have to pry it out of her hands. I vow she has read it a hundred times. And she very rarely goes out these days. I try not to ask too much of her."

Mrs. Kingsley nodded, sympathy plain to read on her face. Everyone felt bad for his mother, for her entire life had crumpled after Father's riding accident.

Diana was deep in conversation with her father, leaving Alec to contemplate his soup. Perfect cubes of carrot floated in it, with a sprig of parsley in the middle.

"Are you about to fall asleep in your soup?" There was a smile in Diana's voice, which meant she had forgiven him for his earlier insult. He had skirted a little too close to the truth with the toffee jibe, and had immediately regretted his words. They both knew how bitter she had become since society's rejection of the Kingsleys, after she jilted Fortescue. Only a dolt would remind her.

He turned to her. "It has been an incredibly long day." Spent on learning how to take care of horses he could neither afford nor afford to keep in the manner to which they had become accustomed.

Much like not being able to ask Diana to marry him, in that respect. He couldn't keep her in the manner to which she had become accustomed, either. *Would you like mutton soup for dinner again? And* of course, *you can have a new dress ... in five years, perhaps.* Not that he hadn't tried.

The truth was Alec had asked Beau Kingsley so many times in the past ten years if he could court Diana, it was a wonder the poor man could see him without running in the opposite direction. His only guess at the denials was that, living so close to them, Diana's father had knowledge of the dire condition of his estate. No man wanted his riches plowed into paying off another man's debt. But of course the good Beau was too polite to say as much, just laughing him off with a "Don't be silly, Templeton. I'm sure you can aim much higher." And on the last occasion, he'd said, "If you must know, I asked her, and she was not entirely keen. Thinks of you as more of a brother, I believe."

It took a while to get over *that* one.

Her gaze quizzed him, a small smile bringing out that winsome dimple in her left cheek. "Poor Templeton, you've run yourself ragged working in the stables. I'm still trying to figure out why."

Alec groaned. His legs hurt like the blazes. "And you'll never know. Tomorrow I may spend the day in the library just to recuperate."

"That sounds lovely. I might join you, unless duty calls me," Diana said.

He dipped his spoon into the soup and lifted it halfway to his mouth. "Duty had better yell. You're notoriously hard of hearing when you read."

She made a choking noise and covered her mouth with her hand. Hopefully, she had not spurted her soup onto the table. He smiled, hoping to fluster her long enough so she would answer his next question without thinking.

"So, Miss Kingsley, how on earth have you become betrothed? Interested parties would like to know." *Interested parties would like to knock the teeth out of the paragon who has offered for you.*

The pain of her failed first engagement had been borne out over the years by her polite rebuff of suitors. No man was a match to that kind of indifference. What on earth had changed? It could only be her new stepmother. Mrs. Cordelia Kingsley would definitely not like sharing the roost with a beautiful but bossy stepdaughter.

She slowly and deliberately put her spoon down and looked at him, her eyes bright with mischief. "Oh, I don't know, he asked, and I said 'yes.' Apparently that's how it works."

Diana Kingsley had always been beautiful to look at, with soft blond hair that curled around her ears, warm caramel eyes, and a long straight nose that was nothing like the potato blob her brother had inherited. She took one's breath away, and that was before she opened her mouth and torched a man with her intelligence. The usual swift stab of guilt at having those thoughts about his best friend's sister shot through him. But then it wasn't like he could act on it, so surely there was no harm?

"I heard no banns. When did you meet this military hero? Pip has told me nothing."

"Perhaps there is not much to tell." She shrugged with none of the wistful expression that he would expect of a bride-to-be. "It was announced in *The Times* three weeks ago. His name is Colonel Webster. He was recently stationed in Malta, but is now entering diplomatic service. Cordelia introduced us a few months ago, as he is a friend of her family. He needs a wife"—she lowered her voice—"and it is my stepmother's belief that I need a husband. That is everything in a nutshell."

Ha! This was no love match. And while it might never be Alec, Diana deserved a love match. Although, who was he to say? Perhaps this was exactly what she wanted. "It sounds like you have the basis for a wonderful union. Will I meet this paragon while I am here? I admit I am very keen to meet the man who has claimed the hand of our fair huntress."

She rolled her eyes and picked up her glass of ratafia, taking a small sip. "I don't know why you call me that."

Perhaps because you look like some mythical goddess who strolled out of the forest, complete with bow and arrow? "Nor I, it just seems to fit."

"You are mad." She returned to the topic at hand. "Colonel Webster is sensible and solid," she said, obviously trying to find exactly the right words to describe her fiancé. "He will do well for me."

"That sounds … interesting," Alec said, quietly because he had no wish for the rest of the table to join in their conversation. "Has he met you? Because I'm not sure how a man who is *sensible* and *solid* would look at *you* and think that you would do well for him." He made sure it sounded as though he put quotation marks around *sensible* and *solid*.

She frowned at him. "I am eminently sensible, I'll have you know. Good sense literally pours through my veins."

"And meets its demise in your head," he replied. "Don't forget, I am the person who watched you dive into a river fully clothed. Fool others, but not your dear Temple."

She rolled her eyes. "I was seven. And you dived in straight after me."

"Have you changed, though? Really?" he said, thoughtful. "For example, what would happen if I reached over and took this lovely pastry?" He reached his hand onto her plate, picked up the morsel, and popped it into his mouth. "Mmm, some kind of meat."

She raised one eyebrow in a beautiful arch. "It is crab meat. And I would just get myself another and chalk the entire experience up to your sad lack of manners."

It was hard to believe that a quiet, solid, and stable man would choose Diana Kingsley for his wife. You only had to be in her company for a quarter-hour to realize she was all fire, spirit and, well, fun. And what of *her*, blast it? What was she going to do with a dirt-boring husband who dragged her to the ends of the earth on diplomatic missions?

He shook his head. This was not his problem. He might never turn his estates around, never be able to support a woman like Diana in the manner she should be supported. "And when are you to be married?"

"Early autumn," Diana said. "He is very busy preparing for his new post. I am, of course, flexible."

"I'm sure you would both just like to get the wedding done with and the marriage started." Alec refused to examine why he felt queasy. It was probably the crab tart. Maybe it had turned. "Well, good luck."

"Don't you mean you wish me happy?"

He quirked an eyebrow. "I think luck is a better thing to wish you. Then the happiness can take care of itself in due course." He pushed his plate away and a footman came to take it almost immediately. "I find I am not hungry tonight." The urge to leave the dinner table entirely was strong, but he made himself stay seated because the last thing he wanted to do was offend Diana twice in one day. Instead, he changed the subject. "Have you heard about the latest gentlemanly race listed at White's?" He raised his voice a little to include everyone.

She seemed as happy as he to leave the topic of her marriage behind. Her eyes twinkled with mischief. "Oh, please, do tell me about it," she said. "You know I love a good race."

She certainly did love a good race. He could remember countless battles in their teenage years when all three of them galloped across the countryside from church steeple to steeple. On one unforgettable afternoon, they raced an approaching storm front. Diana was a bruising rider and well suited to any conditions the English countryside and weather could throw at her.

"Well," he said with relish. "It is quite the talk of the town. The Prince of Wales himself has created a sweepstake and left the entries open to as many drivers as have the hundred guinea entry fee, which he will then match. The race is to go between London and Brighton for the opening of the prince's new stables, the winner taking the entire purse, which could be thousands of guineas, depending on how many carriages enter."

She blinked. "Thousands of guineas, you say. That *is* quite enthralling." She sat for a few moments, looking down, and he tried not to notice, but her bosom was rising and falling very quickly. Why would the thought of a big prize make the wealthy Diana Kingsley so excited?

"How can they possibly do that on the Brighton Road?" Mrs. Kingsley interrupted. "You can't clog the major thoroughfare with sporting curricles! The magistrates won't hear of it!"

Pip took the question with relish. "Apparently, the race is to be a time trial with drivers leaving sporadically from seven in the morning. Quite safe, and stewards at each change. I believe the magistrates have been informed. It will all be taken care of."

Mrs. Kingsley lifted her chin in the air. "Well, I think it's madness. Like those gentlemen who think it's a great lark to commandeer mail coaches and the such." The small fern on her headpiece quivered.

Diana ignored that remark and turned to him. "Are you entering?"

He would if he had a spare hundred guineas to squander. "I might."

She nodded. "You should. You are an excellent whip. Perhaps I shall travel to Brighton to be at the finish line. How exciting." The bosom was no longer rising and falling. She had reined herself in and dampened her excitement. *It would never do.* She should never have to be less than she was.

He lowered his voice, making sure Mrs. Kingsley was occupied with her husband. "Be at the finish line? Why would you want to do something so pedestrian? Why wouldn't you race?"

"Surely only gentlemen can race?" Her eyes flashed in excitement again.

He had spiked her interest, wedding be damned. "I read the rules carefully at White's, and let me tell you, they mentioned nothing about being a gentleman. All it stipulated was 'driver.'"

Her mouth formed a perfect *O* of surprise. "Do you think ladies will enter?"

He shrugged his shoulders. "Any lady clever enough to read

between the lines, and any lady who has a gentleman friend who tells her of this wording, might enter. As long, I suppose, as her fiancé has no qualms about her entering."

She said nothing, but apparently, the soup was no longer to her taste either because she also pushed her bowl away. "I'm sure I have too many things to do, preparing for the wedding, without entering a silly carriage race."

"Of course. Perhaps I will race for both of us. Because I not only want to, I could use the funds." Which was a grand understatement. Without the funds he could not start his breeding enterprise, even in a small way, and certainly couldn't assuage the many creditors that trudged their way to Althorne on a regular basis.

"Been gambling again?" she asked innocently.

It might have been an impertinent thing to say, but it warmed Alec's heart because it meant his efforts to appear wealthy still worked. In truth, the idea of gambling away what little he had made him feel sick to the stomach. He could never be so foolhardy.

The land he lived on, the hereditary lands of the Earls Templeton, were mortgaged so far that every scrap of income that came in had to be given to the bank, or the moneylenders, or towards the rest of the pile of debts his father had left him. And that was before he even thought of the backlog of maintenance the estates required.

"Oh, yes, gambling," he said easily, "or buying new boots or a new phaeton—a man has to keep up, doesn't he?"

Keeping up with Prinny meant his father's wardrobe had been worth a small fortune. Alec had sold every last stitch.

It made nothing more than a wee dent in the debt.

She shook her head. "I don't know, Templeton. I think it would be more prudent for a man to live within his means. But if anybody is well suited for tearing to Brighton and winning thousands of guineas, I'm sure it's you."

And there was the rub. This race seemed like a gamble worth taking. "I certainly hope you're right, Miss Kingsley. Because I would dearly love that large stash of coin."

"I've a mind to enter too," Pip said from across the table, loudly enough that he drew a glare from his stepmother.

Diana smiled. "Pip, you can't even beat me driving to the village. What makes you think you can win in a race with England's best whips?"

Her brother waggled his eyebrows. "I seem to remember a day when I won a race," he said.

Diana smiled broadly at her brother, her dimple making a show again. He adored that mischievous dimple.

"Oh, yes," Alec said. "The famous race to Bradbury, where Diana's curricle ended up in a ditch and I stopped to help, so you drove past us both like a madman to win."

"You both continue to forget that I avoided the ditch *and* Diana," Pip said. "And sink me if I don't think this race is going to have more than a few dirty players in it," he said. "All that money means people will behave badly. This race is going to be just as much about being smart as it is about being fast."

"If we try, we might have a few smart moves of our own," Diana said.

Alec turned to her. "And tell me, what smart moves would you make?"

"Don't tell him, Di," Pip said. "Those moves are for *me*."

Diana turned to Alec. "As my brother rightly says, my smart moves are for him." Lord help him, she matched the statement with a slow wink that nobody but he would notice. His heart lurched, hoping for a flirtation where there likely was none.

"Humph, I'll leave you in the ditch next time." He folded his arms and turned away from her. Even Mrs. Kingsley laughed.

Diana placed her hand on his arm softly, but he felt the heat of it all the way to his impoverished heart. "I'll help you, too. Just differently to Pip."

He nodded, knowing that while Pip might think she was joking, she was in earnest and would help him in any way she could. "I am in your debt, Miss Kingsley."

"You know I like it that way," Diana said, matching her words with a mischievous smile.

CHAPTER 3

IN WHICH DIANA FINDS THE MEMORY IS NOT AS FUNNY AS IT FELT AT THE TIME

Three days later, late summer rain battered the dining-room window where Diana and her stepmother Cordelia had empty vases lined up along the table and a basket of hot-house flowers to arrange in them. It was barely ten in the morning, but Diana took a candle from the sconce and lit the candelabra. "Shall I call someone to light the fire?"

Cordelia nodded, focused on poking pink dahlias around the white salvia. Today, she wore a green turban with a large silk poppy on top. Her silver hair was artfully curled at the front, framing her face. She was dressed as though waiting for company, in a matching green day dress that was caught under her slender bosom with a velvet ribbon. She was surely as fashionable at fifty as she was at twenty-one, perhaps because, as she was wont to say, "I may not have been blessed with children, but at least I have my figure."

Father had married Cordelia six months after the disaster of Fortescue, when word about town had been that Diana's behavior was because of a lack of "gentle influence." She had family connections with Colonel Webster's uncle, the Duke of Wellsmore, which nobody was allowed to forget. In retrospect,

Diana realized Cordelia was Father's first attempt to repair the damage she had done.

"I'm glad you decided against that walk, even if the colonel hasn't arrived yet."

Diana did not wonder out loud what made him late, for Cordelia would just come to his defense and caution Diana not to have expectations of a gentleman, which apparently "only leads to disappointment." And since that kind of proclamation was annoying, she tamped down her irritation and ventured the complete opposite of her thoughts. "I'm sure he will get here when the time is right for him."

Cordelia pursed her mouth. "I would prefer he kept to his promised time, so that my planning with Cook does not go to naught for another night! All that beautiful food and only Lord Templeton to enjoy it."

Diana almost dropped the lit candle on the carpet, then looked around the room to see if anyone else had witnessed this complete reversal of opinion. But, no, they were alone.

Colonel Webster was supposed to arrive late on Wednesday evening, but it was already Thursday morning, and there was still no sign of him. "Well, whatever the reason, I do wish he would come soon."

She must have sounded enthusiastic because Cordelia looked up from her arrangement and smiled. "I am so pleased to hear that. He is a wonderful match, and I will be forever happy to have thought of it!"

Diana didn't have the heart to admit she only awaited his arrival in order to banish the anxiety Templeton had created by talking about him. With each answer she gave him, he was increasingly dubious. It was in his expression. And that made her question her own judgment in the matter. And without Colonel Webster there, there was nothing to stop the runaway carriage of her mind. Which, she supposed, was the problem when one conducted a marriage of practicality rather than of the heart.

She tried, unsuccessfully, to remember exactly what it was about him that had led her to accept his proposal.

It wasn't the usual courtship niceties, the visits and flowers where he displayed his beautiful manners. Might it have been the chance to travel the world and see something other than England? He hoped to stay in postings only a short while and travel the world on His Majesty's service. The thought of visiting foreign lands was appealing. But what if she didn't like it? Then she would be stuck in a country where she knew no one, didn't speak the language, and was far away from everyone she loved. And possibly in a delicate condition, to boot. *That* thought kept her awake for *hours*.

In retrospect, accepting an offer because your father looked so incredibly happy about it might not have been entirely logical.

Please let him quell these anxious thoughts that race around my mind. He had that kind of calm and steadying influence. Maybe *that* was why she had said yes. The past months had found her becoming increasingly jittery, like there was an urgent need that she *do* something. *Do what though?*

She wanted to see new horizons, and the moment he announced his next posting was in Calcutta, part of her had decided she would marry him and go too.

She snipped off the long stem of a rose. *What a terrible reason to marry a man.*

Please, Lord, let him come soon and allay my fears.

"I had a letter from cousin Sophia yesterday," Cordelia began, her eyes on her floral arrangement. Cousin Sophia was not really a cousin, but the aunt of her former husband and the Duke of Wellsmore's sister. Therefore, in Cordelia's eyes, the most important of connections. "She wishes you well and would like to know the date of the upcoming ceremony."

Diana's chest tightened. "We do not yet have a date." Perhaps when they set a date, she would feel more settled.

Cordelia nodded. "I know. But I think it would be prudent to name one with the colonel's visit. It is time to make more definite plans. Although, I think a small wedding would be preferable. I'm sure you will agree." She didn't have to say "after last time," but the words still hung in the air like a miasma.

Her previous betrothal had run into problems a mere two days before the wedding.

Diana had been in an adjoining room, taking tea with her aunts when the men came in from their cricket match. Her young self had blushed when she heard them teasing her soon-to-be husband about being caught in the "parson's trap."

Lord Fortescue had laughed good-naturedly. "I keep telling myself it will be worth it."

"And you get the lovely Miss Kingsley," someone had said. "Lady Luck herself in your pocket. Cheer up!"

"I suppose she will come in handy to run my stables for me."

She still remembered the sharp intake of breath between her aunts, and the blush running up her cheeks like a furious fire. It sounded like marrying her was for nothing more than getting a good stablehand.

"And I hear you're getting Equinox in her dowry," a more familiar voice had said. It was her brother's best friend, the Earl of Templeton.

"I *demanded* that I get him in her dowry," her fiancé had said. "If that horse isn't in my stable after the ceremony, there will be words. I mean, let's be frank. Why else would I want to get leg-shackled? You gentlemen think me a ninny, but believe me I am the furthest thing from that."

"He only got the license to get it over with as quickly as possible," said someone she didn't recognize.

"No calling of the banns here," he laughed easily. "If I had to draw it out over a few weeks, I might back out."

"Not while I live and breathe," Aunt Victoria had said. "He can't mean that."

"And what if he does?" Aunt Philippa replied, ever practical. "What can we do now, so close to the wedding?"

There was a scuffle and some shouting and then Fortescue said, "Templeton, you dog. You almost broke my jaw!"

Later she had found out Templeton had punched him, leaving a bruise that lasted weeks. The first and only time a man went into battle for her. She liked to imagine that punch as if she'd done it herself. It always sent a thrill up her spine.

Aunt Philippa had patted Diana on the shoulder. "I daresay once he gets to know Diana, he will change his tune. She will make a wonderful wife."

Would she? Diana's saucer shook in her hand with the teacup rattling on top of it. She put it down on the side table before she lost complete control and spilled tea all over her beautiful new dress. Her mind still could not comprehend what he was saying. Did he really mean he did not love her? How could this be true? She had felt the need to be alone. Fast. Aunt Victoria, ever the voice of reason, stood up.

"Come, Diana. We should get you upstairs to rest. We had enough excitement for today. Gentlemen say the craziest things sometimes amongst their friends. I'm sure Aunt Philippa agrees?"

She murmured her agreement, but along with the murmur there was a shared look that Diana could not miss. What he had said *was* wrong and *did* reflect badly on her.

What he had said made him the last person on earth she would ever marry.

It had been two days until the wedding.

Hurt to the core, Diana was grateful for the outraged thoughts, which were running through a list of suitable retributions, instead of listening to her heart. It wanted to quietly keen in a corner.

Diana had forced a smile at her aunts, her mind still racing. "Diana, don't."

She pushed past them. "Don't what?"

"Whatever it is you're thinking of doing. He didn't mean it. It was just silly bravado. And in any case, what marriage starts off with love? These things build over years, not months. Once he knows you better, he will love you. How could he not?"

Diana sat back in her chair, her course of action decided. She picked up her teacup again, and this time the saucer did not rattle. "Please do not worry about me. I will handle the situation as I see fit."

Aunt Philippa had raised her eyebrows. "I don't trust this, Vicky."

"She knows her duty," Aunt Victoria had replied with some pride. Misplaced, as it turned out.

Pride in her sister's only daughter marrying a man who did not value her. It boggled one's mind. Duty be damned. She couldn't care less if her father needed the connection with the marquess.

Diana had managed to hoodwink them all for those two days.

When she chose to have her groom ride Equinox alongside her wedding carriage, nobody thought anything of it. Even her father had thought it a lovely touch. At her insistence, he had even agreed to let her have a few minutes with the horse before the ceremony, while he went inside to check all was well.

But when the horse was slapped on the rump by Diana and sent down the aisle on his own at St. George's Hanover Square, with flowers and ribbons threaded through his glossy black mane and a note around his neck that read, *You wanted to marry a horse. Here, have at it.* There was an uproar about *that*.

And heaven help her, the first thing she thought as her carriage ripped down Grosvenor Street toward Hyde Park was, *Will Alec follow me?* Images of running away with him in her wedding finery had been the only thing that held her together.

He did not.

〜

"Wool gathering?" Cordelia said, interrupting the less than pleasant memory with a soft smile. "Thinking about one's husband-to-be is one of the most exciting parts of getting married. I would envy you if I weren't so happily situated myself. One is never too old to love again. We are both proof of that, Diana."

Diana was proof of many things. That the mistakes made in youth could haunt a body like a specter. That nothing good came of headstrong young ladies.

But that one was never too old to love again?

Unlikely.

"I am also very proud that you did not make a fuss about not entering the race last night at dinner. I know what a good whip you are and how much you enjoy a challenge. It is part of the reason I put you forward as a match for Colonel Webster. You will put those traits to good use when you are his wife. Your father will be proud, if I may be so bold as to say."

"That will be a lovely change for him," Diana said mildly. The more time passed, the easier it was to say something that stung like a wasp in the most ladylike of tones. Somebody should list *that* as an accomplishment.

But Cordelia was wrong if she thought Diana wasn't upset about not entering the race. She hid her true feelings beneath a mountain of demure nods and smiles. But under all that, the thought of the race thrummed in her veins like music in the background one could not quite name.

She was just trying to figure out how to make it happen without risking everything she'd gained back.

CHAPTER 4

After Diana left Cordelia, she went to the library to find Pip so they could talk about the race.

The rain had cleared and Cordelia was happy with Diana, not only because the floral arrangements were dotted around the house, but she had also done an hour's worth of embroidery on a tablecloth that was to go in her wedding chest.

The sun broke through the clouds, bathing the library in soft, golden light and warming it as much as the fire that burned in the grate. The room smelled of books, leather, and the beeswax that was used on the tables. But something else was in the air, something light and citrus in flavor. She frowned and looked around. No Pip.

But in the corner, sitting at the desk near the window, with a book and a quill in his hands, was the Earl of Templeton. His pale-blue coat hung on the back of a chair, with his cravat loose and his sleeves rolled up. His forearms were as brown and muscled as you would expect from a man who rode and lived an active life.

The breath caught in her chest, and she tore her eyes away from them.

He looked up from his book and smiled. "Good afternoon. As you see, I am making good on my promise not to work." He leaned back in his chair and stretched. "I do not possess a muscle that is not currently complaining most bitterly about my treatment of it."

Diana stepped into the room. "Hard work will do that."

"If you're looking for your brother, I'm afraid he is off finding us more tea and hopefully bread. Teaching thick-headed me has made him hungry." He picked up his quill and looked back at his book, as if their conversation were over.

"He lives in a state of perpetual famishment," she said, lifting a book from the pile next to him and turning it to read the spine. She sat her bottom on the edge of the desk, exactly as she would if Father were sitting there, or Pip.

Templeton stilled, then blinked slowly. His dark eyelashes were thick and long, in a way any lady would envy, and his gaze was stuck at the spot where she sat. Then he jolted back his chair to increase the space between them.

Diana didn't move, not wanting to acknowledge whatever had made *him* move. Was it her? She dropped her head to her arm. Perhaps her dress smelled stale? No, it did not. Which could only mean it was her closeness that had that effect on him. Her breath caught in her throat. *Oh.*

"I've heard stories about your days at Eton," she said mildly. "In none of those stories were you *ever* scholarly."

He crossed his arms over his chest and leaned back in his chair. "When it is boring Greek or Latin, I have always been unenthused. However, your father's library on horse rearing and breeding is likely without parallel in England." He thought about it for a moment. "Probably the world."

She stood quickly, finding it hard to hide her astonishment. "I did *not* know you were interested in breeding. I thought you were just amusing yourself." Men like him, who had been surrounded by luxury and wealth, rarely liked the practical hard work that horse breeding took. Unlike Father who, despite being of the landed gentry, knew how to clean out a stall.

"I always have been, but it was not something my father allowed me to indulge." He paused briefly, and with a sad look between them, they acknowledged it was a bitter thing to have to lose a parent to follow one's heart's desire. "However, I have a small stable of breeding horses, and I would dearly like to start my own stud."

Now, finding him in the stables made sense. He loved horses as much as she or Pip, so it was a natural progression. But it also flew in the face of everything society thought it knew about him. That he was just an extravagant wastrel following in his father's ruinous footsteps. *Really, though, had that ever felt right?*

The fact that he was doing exactly what *she* would do if she were a man only elevated him in her estimation. "Well, Templeton, you have supporters in the very best family you could for this endeavor. My father will be happy to help you. In fact, I would be more than happy to help you myself," she said. "I know as much as Pip and, while not as much as Father, I am perhaps a little more modern in my approach. I may have my downfall in watercolors, but when it comes to rearing horses, I am a lady of accomplishment."

It was a shame more of society didn't think so. All they seemed to value was hours of valuable time practicing the harp.

Pip came back a few moments later, carrying a tray laden with scones, followed by a maid who was carrying a bowl of jam and one of cream. The scones still had steam rising from them.

Pip's brown hair was ruffled like he'd been running his hands through it, and his cravat was undone. His usual messy self, in other words.

Everything about him was from their mother's side of the family, the Ryecrofts. Solidly built, clear gray eyes, and an abiding love of good food. He was a dutiful spaniel where Templeton was more of a wolfhound, imposing and mysterious. *Not* that she should be comparing men to dogs.

"These will entice me to stay with you gentlemen for a few moments more," Diana said. "Pip, you have a sixth sense for when Cook is baking."

"It's not a sixth, more like the third. I just use my nose," Pip said. "She said they were not for breakfast, but I think they taste divine any time of day."

Diana took one, adding a thick dollop of jam and then cream. "Templeton told me he is going to start a horse breeding stud, and you are teaching him. A fine enterprise."

Pip hadn't mentioned it to her, keeping Templeton's plans secret like a good and loyal friend. However, the smile on his face suggested he was happy the news was out in the open, where he could share everything with his sister, as he normally did.

"It's like being able to do everything Father told us we couldn't, and it's so exciting. You remember that idea I had for selectively breeding both mare and stallion?"

Diana nodded. It had been a wonderful idea, but entirely too progressive for their traditional father. "And he will probably be the first one interested to see how that unfolds. He just doesn't want to be the one to put his neck out and try it." If only she could be involved, too. But that was not a woman's lot. Or, at least, not hers.

"Exactly!" Pip said. "I asked him … well, actually, Temple asked him if he could work around the stables for a few months, and he agreed. It's going to take some time for Temple to come up with the blunt to establish his stable, and in the meantime he can be learning."

"I'm not afraid to get my hands dirty," Templeton said.

Diana nodded. "'Tis the truth. I've seen him with mud from the tips of his toes to the top of his head. Remember that time you tumbled over that fence and straight into a bog?"

Templeton made an exasperated huff. "Miss Kingsley, why is

it you always seem to remember my most embarrassing moments?"

Diana smiled and then moved on to the topic she had come to the library for. She turned to her brother. "I need a promise from you."

"Anything, you know it," Pip said, not even asking what she wanted a promise for.

Diana smiled. Other brothers were spiteful or uncaring creatures, but he was her champion. "I am going to help you with your race, but if you win, will you use the winnings to help me buy Equinox back from the prince? Father may be mad, but then he will truly be ours."

Pip nodded. "A worthy cause. I will."

Templeton held up a hand. "Hold on a moment. Do you mean to tell me you are not racing?"

"How can she? Don't be daft." Pip reached out to clip his friend over the ears, but Templeton dodged it.

She shook her head. "I am not racing. I am planning. I will be somewhere along the race route to support you both on the day." If she could manage it. It would take careful negotiation with Cordelia and Father.

Templeton looked at her in astonishment. Then he turned to Pip. "When I let slip to your sister that the rules of the race do not bar ladies from entering, I was sure she'd be at the starting line with us."

Pip minutely shook his head. "I know you like to think she is still the scapegrace of our childhood, but, believe me, society has unfortunately taught her some hard lessons. If she is not racing, it is not because she couldn't beat us all but because she would never live it down."

Diana nodded, her heart warm at how well Pip understood. "I am being prudent for once in my life. I would like to share my ideas with you. Where shall we go? You can bring your scones with you."

"Why the secrecy? I thought you were going to help me, too?" Templeton said.

She sighed, eyeing him with her best stern governess look. "Goodness, you sound like a whining babe. Of course I will help you. Come to me later and I'll give you precise directions on some changes to your carriage you need to make."

"I live to eat the crumbs you drop me," he said, bowing and giving her his most flirtatious smile. Her heart thudded a little harder and faster.

"As it should be," she replied, raising her nose in the air like the haughtiest duchess.

Templeton stood and picked up his coat. "You two stay here. I've finished my lessons for the day and might visit the stables."

CHAPTER 5

IN WHICH DIANA HITS THE BULLSEYE

Kingsley Estate was at its best in summer, when the horses at pasture lazed under trees, and the foals were old enough to frolic around them. Beau Kingsley liked to have them born in late spring and early summer, when the grasses grew strongest, so the mothers would have good milk.

The burning question, Alec thought, lying on his back and looking up into the leafy canopy of an old oak, had nothing to do with horses and everything to do with how long he could stay at Kingsley with both Diana and her fiancé in residence.

It made him itchy enough with Diana around, reminding him every day of what equal amounts of perfection and mischief looked like. Imagine throwing the man who had been deemed worthy of her into the mix?

Especially if they looked even *remotely* like they were in love.

Unbearable.

When she'd sat on the desk yesterday, and his hand ended up a few inches from her, it had been everything he could do to stay sane. In that elongated moment, with her bottom right in front of him, something snapped inside. For a frightening second, he'd almost given in to the impulse to reach out and touch her. Her closeness, the very fragrance of her, was intoxicating.

He'd always loved her. But now it hurt, too, in a painful gut-wrenching way. *Leave before you do something stupid.*

The leaves rustled above him, and the breeze caressed his face like a balm. He took a deep breath. *It will all be fine.* She would go off to Istanbul or some other far-flung corner of the globe, and he would go on.

The sound of swishing muslin had him lifting his head to see Diana stride across the field in front of him. She carried her bow and had a leather quiver slung across her back. It made sense, as this tree was right next to the archery range. Only a slight breeze from the west rustled the leaves on the trees, and the range was in a slight hollow, protecting it even further. A perfect day for it. He supposed he should be grateful she was not practicing her pistol shooting, something she was equally good at.

Head down and deep in thought, she did not see him. He did not raise a hand or his voice to greet her, but watched her sling arrows at the target.

Twang. Whistle. Thump.

Twang. Whistle. Thump.

The sound went on for some time, because heaven knew Diana had always found satisfaction in putting a hole in inanimate objects.

He lifted his head. She took an arrow from her quiver, pulled her bow back, and launched it at the target, missing the small circle in the middle, and all the other circles around it.

Another.

Missed again.

"Drat," she cursed under her breath.

He sat up. "You should try not to grip the bow so hard," he said.

She started and gave a little yelp. "And you should try not to scare a body like that. I could easily have shot you!"

"You? Shoot that far from the mark? Unlikely."

"Well, I will not keep going now I know I have an audience." Dressed in a delightful white muslin that was not made for archery, she planted one hand on her hip, the other holding her bow. Her hair had abandoned any attempt at confinement and curled around her head in a golden halo. *And she wonders why I call her my huntress?*

"Or I could join you instead." He strolled over to her and took the bow. "Now let's see … It's been a while."

"You have it the wrong way around." She reached to move the bow but found his hand instead. The world slowed as her hand brushed his, and he felt the small touch all the way to his toes.

"Ah, yes. Of course." *Deep breath, Alec.* He took an arrow from her, placed it on the bow, lifted and released in one fluid movement that spoke of the many days he'd spent practicing as a boy.

He hit the target but not the bullseye.

"I feel better now," she said.

He smiled, loving her humor. "Another person failing can have that effect. Perhaps I should stick to horse breeding."

She took the bow from him. "I am *most* impressed by what you are trying to achieve. Are your stables set up?"

He nodded. "My father spent a lot on them. I have spent nothing." Not that he had reserves *to* spend.

"It doesn't matter how old they are, if they are still warm and dry. Room for how many?"

"Twenty."

"Enough to get you started." She released an arrow, which landed closer to the bullseye. "How far are you from launching?"

"I can start now, just not on a grand scale. I got a broodmare called Penelope from the Duke of Grafton last month." It was actually quite a coup. He'd sold paintings from the gallery and used everything on hand to secure the mare with impeccable bloodlines.

"Oh, *very* nice. Well done. She was strong a few years ago at Newmarket. A beautiful girl. Her dam was Prunella, I think?" She took another shot, then, having run out of arrows, strode toward the target before pulling each arrow out and putting them back in her quiver.

How many people in the country would know what a triumph it was for him to negotiate Penelope away from Grafton? Much less who the horse's mother was? A handful, no more.

When she returned, she was deep in thought. "What do you think of Ned?"

"He's a genius." Ned was the Kingsley trainer, who could get a horse to do anything and would do anything for a horse.

"You need someone like him if you're serious."

Of course he did. But wanting a Ned wasn't as easy as finding one. "They don't grow thick on the ground, you know."

"Only too well. But he has a son. Artie. He's only fifteen, but will be starting work soon. You should speak to Ned and see if you can offer Artie a job." She bit her thumb. "Before Father does, although you didn't hear that from me."

"But he's just a boy. Surely ..."

She shook her head. "He's Ned's son and, if I had to take a guess, I'd say he is everything his father is and more. Plus, he won't be as set against new ways as Ned is."

He took a deep breath. She was right; Artie would be a perfect employee. "I'll speak to him this afternoon. Thank you. I don't know what I'm going to do when you leave."

She threw him a mischievous smile. "Fail miserably, I have no doubt."

"Ah, if only we lived in a world where I could have you with me forever, to give me unsolicited advice and save my hide over and over."

She notched an arrow in her bow and pulled back on the

string. "That's called marriage, Templeton, and you have thus far managed to evade it." She released the arrow, and it sailed toward the target, hitting the center of the bullseye.

"Bravo, my dear," a deep voice said from behind them.

CHAPTER 6

IN WHICH AN ENGAGEMENT HINGES ON A HORSE'S FEELINGS

Diana whirled around. "Colonel Webster!" It was hard to say whether the thumping of her heart was happiness at his arrival, or horror at being caught half-flirting with Templeton when he did. "You are here at last. I am so glad. How was your trip?" One thing was for certain; his presence brought none of the instant calm she had hoped for.

"Clive," he corrected her. "And it was perfect in every way, especially when the destination was you. My apologies for being a day late." He took off his hat, revealing thinning brown hair with a touch of gray at his temples. He was a little shorter than Diana, but not so much that it made a difference.

"Ha," she said, delighted. "Very gallant."

Then she remembered her manners. "Lord Templeton, may I present Colonel Clive Webster?" She was sure an earl outranked the nephew of a duke, but hoped she had offended no one.

Templeton bowed. "An honor to meet you, sir." He then bowed to Diana. "I will take my leave of you. I hope to see you both at dinner?"

"Certainly, Lord Templeton." She curtsied to him.

She should not be relieved that Templeton took such a quick

departure, but surely any conversation between the three of them would have been either embarrassing or awkward. Or both. Templeton knew her in a way that her fiancé hopefully never would.

Colonel Webster wore a dark-navy coat with gold buttons that were emblazoned with eagles, buckskin breeches, and hessians she could see her reflection in if she looked hard enough. His cravat was a crisp and snowy fold that looked just tied. All of which added up to a man who took great care in his toilette before presenting himself. Diana tucked a loose curl behind her ear. He must have changed before coming to meet her. Being almost forty, he did not quite have a young man's body, but he was still tall enough to carry off the breeches and sporting attire. She thought the silver in his hair gave him a great air of distinction.

He took her hand and raised it to his lips, brushing the leather of her glove lightly. "Could I tempt you to come for a drive with me? I have had your grooms hitch a couple of horses up to a nice sporting curricle I spied when I came in."

"Ah, yes, that will be Father's last birthday present," she said. "You must be a great favorite, if he is letting you drive it."

He laughed. "The grooms had to get permission, you're right! Shall we?"

Her whole person was heated, and there was a grass stain on her white gown. But that was nothing to the feeling she just needed a moment to calm her fluster. "If you will allow me a moment to repair myself? You could meet me at the front of the house in a quarter of an hour?"

"Of course." He took Diana's arm, and they walked across the grass toward the stables. Balancing her bow and quiver, she tried to tidy her curls, which had become an unruly mess.

He smiled, his voice calm and amused. "Here, give me that. And you are perfectly fine, just as you are. I would not change a hair on your head. But take as long as you need. I will be waiting."

Oh. She took a deep breath, and the tightness in her stomach unraveled. "You are very kind. Thank you." He always said the right things at the right times. Part of being a diplomat, she supposed, always knowing how to smooth the waters and make people feel at ease.

She went to her room and repaired the damage to her hair and dress, dabbed cold water on her face with a linen towel, and made her way back downstairs, an elegant shawl draped around her shoulders. Much improved from the bow-slinging hoyden he had encountered a few minutes ago.

As promised, he was waiting out the front with her father's curricle, teamed with Whinny and Whicker, two of her favorite chestnuts.

"Hello, Whinny," she said, giving her a gentle rub behind the ear. "How has your morning been?" The horse nuzzled her, and Diana stroked her neck and then allowed herself to be handed into the curricle by Colonel Webster.

He checked the equipage quickly. *Good work, Colonel. A good driver always makes sure all is in order.* Then he jumped up himself, taking a firm grip on the reins. Did he tug too sharply at the reins to set them off? Perhaps. But each driver was a little different in the way he handled his team. Unfortunately, it would never do for Whinny and Whicker.

She touched his arm. "These are gentle creatures, Colonel. A very light hand is all they need."

He darted a surprised look at her criticism, a grimace of embarrassment appearing before he blinked and smoothed his expression. "My apologies. It has been quite some time since I drove a sporting vehicle. I must be nervous."

Diana smiled indulgently. That was perhaps the only excuse she would accept for his clumsiness. "Would you like me to take them? I know the horses and the roads intimately."

His cheeks colored red. "I am perfectly capable of driving these horses, never fear."

Oh dear. She had stepped on his pride—a common mistake for her with any man—although this was the first time with him.

"Of course you are. I was not intimating otherwise. I have complete trust in you." This was not quite true, because she did not have complete trust in anyone but herself. And of course, her father and Pip. The trust probably extended to Templeton. But no one else.

Colonel Webster treated the horses gently from there on out, shooting glances at her every once in a while, perhaps just to see if she was paying attention, which she most certainly was.

He relaxed back into the seat. "I suppose being Beau Kingsley's daughter means you have done a great deal of riding and driving."

She nodded. "I rode before I could walk and my father taught me to drive on my twelfth birthday."

"I am sure it is just one of many of your accomplishments," he said.

And while that was a lovely compliment, all she could think was that he was trying to win back her favor after he had so swiftly lost it. "In truth, I don't have many accomplishments," she replied. "Watercolor, needlework, or even the pianoforte, do not interest me. I have rudimentary skills in all but archery. I am an excellent archer. I'm afraid my childhood was spent scampering around the countryside, chasing my brother hither and thither, riding horses or taking care of horses. There was little time for anything else, much to my mother's chagrin. Then when she died, there was no one to stop me."

He laughed as though she were joking. "There now, I'm sure once we marry, it will be quite the opposite—no time for riding and all the time in the world to improve your domestic skills."

Diana's head tilted to the side of its own volition as she tried to understand him. Did he think she was embarrassed by her lack of ladylike skills? "Right, yes. So much time for domestic skills." Her stomach twisted at the thought, because all she could think was that when one *domesticated* an animal, one tamed it, or brought it to heel. *No, thank you.*

They soon left the expansive Kingsley estate and were trotting along the lane that led to the local village. Colonel Webster pulled hard to the right on Whinny's bit, and she reacted just as Diana thought she would, by stopping completely, creating a great awkwardness until Whicker stopped too.

"Dear me, they are quite precocious," he said gruffly, lifting his whip.

Don't you dare!

She put her hand on his arm to stop him. "No, actually, she just needs to be treated gently. Do not use that whip on her unless it is with the softest tickle. All you'll achieve is to make her anxious, which I can assure you, she already is. She needs to be whispered to just as you would a child. Then she will reward you with a wonderful ride."

He nodded. "Of course. You must understand, my usual mounts are used to war times when shouting to be heard above the din was the order of the day." He laughed. "I have to smack my Phineas on the rump to have him do anything!"

I think not! Her mouth pursed in anger at the thought of anyone laying a hand on dear Whinny. "I would encourage you never to try that on a Kingsley horse. Gently, like this." She spoke soft and encouraging words to both horses, and soon they were on their way again.

I should not have to tell you these things was what she truly wanted to say. Every good rider and good driver should know them. Caring for horses was not just something people should do out of love for them; it was the practical thing to do, if you wanted to bring out the best in them. But at least he seemed to take her instruction well. Many would not.

Because if he didn't, then perhaps Templeton was right, and he was not the right man for her. Had Templeton said that? Maybe he just inferred it. Why had she never seen Colonel Webster riding or driving before? Surely she would have noticed his disregard for his mount? If a man disregarded his mount, would he show the same disregard for his wife and children one day?

"Your brother was talking about the race he wants to enter, when I arrived," Colonel Webster said, in a valiant attempt to change the topic.

She allowed it, but only because she desperately needed time to think. "I believe it is a hundred-guinea entry fee. I do wonder where Pip will find that kind of money."

"I am sure he will rustle it up. I also heard Lord Templeton say *you* should enter the race, if you can believe it." He laughed, as though it were the funniest thing he'd heard all day.

Diana did not. "I can well believe it. I bested both of them so many times in our youth, he likely believes I have a good chance of bringing home the purse. Would you like me to race, if it meant I brought an extra thousand guineas to our marriage?"

It was not something she would ever have brought up of her own accord, but the question now hung there like a ripe apple. And she found she wanted him to say "yes," even if his reasons were purely mercenary.

Instead, he shuddered in a horror that was reflected in his pale-blue eyes. "It would scare me witless if you entered a race like that. Templeton must be mad to encourage you."

Diana ignored that piece of foolery. "It will be interesting to see if any ladies enter. Apparently, there has been no stipulation about the gender of the entrants."

He huffed. "Indeed, I'm sure they assume only gentlemen would enter, and as soon as it becomes apparent a lady has entered, they will rewrite the rules before you can say 'ready, steady, go.'" He looked imploringly at her. "A race like that is no place for a gently bred lady."

She hated the way men were allowed to do whatever they wanted, while women had to beg for permission. Mens' independence celebrated, theirs quashed. Mens' forthrightness indulged, women's outlawed. All the way to marriage, when women were seen as an asset to be bargained.

Diana couldn't help herself, she had to ask. "Why not? If the horses and roads are equal, surely a woman can drive just as well as a man." He nodded. "I think it's safe to say that you drive better than I, and probably most of the men I know."

She relaxed a little at the compliment. If he could admit her skill, perhaps she was doing him a disservice. "Thank you."

"But who will protect you during the race? Who will make sure no harm befalls you? You are much too precious. I know you are not seriously thinking about it, but if you were, I would urge caution and prudence."

She smiled brightly. "My dear Colonel Webster, of *course*, I'm not." *Oh, just you telling me I should not means I most definitely am. Especially if it means I can buy my Equinox back.*

He nodded, not knowing her well enough to read her tone. "Good, let's leave it at that. After all, neither of us has any need for the money."

Father had assured her Colonel Webster was well situated, and in receipt of five thousand a year in addition to the forty thousand her dowry would bring. Perhaps there was an easier way to have Equinox back at her side. "I have a question. I hope you do not think me impudent."

"How could I?" Keeping his eyes on the team, he lifted her hand and brought it to his lips.

He let her hand back down, and she clasped it in her lap, not sure why his touch felt so alien. "Would you consider buying Equinox back from the Prince of Wales, as a wedding present to me?"

The reins slackened, but he quickly recovered them. "The horse your father has just sold?"

"The very same. You see, I love him most dearly." It cost her something to say that, like she had laid herself bare to him without quite meaning to.

He looked at her, eyebrows raised in astonishment. "But, my dear, how could we possibly take the best care of him when we are at our postings around the world? To truly care for him, you must put his comfort first, no? And where better for him to be than in the most beautiful stables in the world?"

He spoke nothing but the truth. But her chest deflated and her shoulders slumped. Her boy. Gone. "I know. I just don't want to lose him."

"Your loyalty does you credit." But his tone suggested the conversation was over.

So much for not changing a hair on her head. That was all very well as long as he liked the hairs and they didn't ask him to do something he didn't want to.

"Perhaps you would like to ride with me tomorrow morning so you can see what a beautiful horse he is?"

"I'm sure he is the most beautiful horse in England. Unfortunately, I am promised a tour of the estate with your father."

Diana nodded. "Very well." Two could play at the diplomatic manipulation game. She already knew of the tour, and the last thing she wanted was him coming along on her ride.

CHAPTER 7

WHERE A FRIEND MAKES ANNOYINGLY GOOD SENSE

Before breakfast the next morning, Diana escaped with Equinox.

He was frisky, tossing his head and being vocal. He definitely wanted a good gallop, which was just as well because she was burning for one too. They flew across the fields together, wind whipping across her face, his steady gait rolling under her like an ocean swell. Her Equinox.

It felt like the last of the summer days. The long grass moving in the wind like the waves of golden sea, a row of gardeners scything it in the distance. But it also felt like everything good was ending and that she was riding to outrun an oncoming storm. But, no, she must not think that way. Her future with a husband could hold just as much beauty, and perhaps even more adventure.

If only she had a better grip on whom he actually was. His manners had been perfect at dinner. He entered the wedding conversation with a spirit of generosity and excitement, even going so far as to offer to look into a marriage license so no banns had to be called. So, what exactly was the problem? The feeling, somehow, that he was three steps ahead of her and leading her through a maze of his own making?

Before she quite understood where she was headed, Equinox took her toward the village and, within a few minutes, he slowed at the gate of the vicarage, which was on the edge of Newmarket.

She rubbed her hand up his neck. "My dear boy, you know just what I need, don't you?"

Diana and Beth had been the best of friends since pulling faces at one another during church services when they were seven. Beth was always welcome at Kingsley House, and at the vicarage, Diana was sure of a cup of tea and the peace that was now missing in her own house since Mama passed away.

Beth and her sister, Bernadette, were tending the garden. Beth had a basket of carrots next to her, while Bernadette was weeding.

"Hello there!" Diana shouted. "How long does a person have to wait for someone to open the gate at this establishment?"

Beth looked up and grinned, running to the gate and then pulling it open. She had a large smudge of dirt on her nose.

"Carrots for dinner?" Diana asked.

Her friend rolled her eyes. "Only every day this week! I'm so glad to see you. This is the perfect excuse for a break."

Bernadette, just turned thirteen, ran into the house, her plaited hair flying out behind her.

"She is probably going to warn mother, who has patterns and pins all over the sitting room."

Diana laughed. "What is she making? Is it the ball gown we bought the blue satin for last week?"

Beth nodded and shrugged. "She seems to think if I wear satin, I might attract more interest. Apparently, it is worth spending five shillings."

Beth's mother had been matchmaking her daughter with any man between eighteen and thirty-five for three years now.

Nobody was immune. Not even the new rector, who definitely had no interest in a wife.

The problem, for Beth, was that she was desperately in love with Pip. It was not something her best friend had ever confided, but one only had to see the way she watched him to divine the truth. Pip, of course, was oblivious to anything that was not a meal set in front of him.

Diana mocked outrage. "You are worth far more than five shillings!" She paused for effect, pretending to think. "I would give you at least ten!"

Beth's eyes danced in delight. "How gracious … I think."

Diana put her hands together in thanks before a thought occurred to her. "But wait! There's some lovely lace trim at home that would work beautifully," Diana said. "Shall I bring it for you tomorrow?"

Beth's eyes widened. Lace was an expensive addition that was moved from dress to dress. "Mother would love nothing more, I'm sure. But why are you here? I am delighted to see you, but weren't we going to meet at the village tomorrow?"

Diana tied Equinox to the tree and took her friend's arm, looping it in hers in it as they walked toward the cottage. "I am in strife, as usual, and need your advice without the prying ears of the village listening in at the haberdashers."

Beth stopped walking and turned to look at her friend. "Then let's not go inside yet. Come, sit with me on our favorite bench."

The rustic bench sat in a small clearing of the herb garden covered by a wooden arch. The enterprising vicar had made it, and Mrs. Harris had trained wisteria over it. For a brief few weeks of summer it was a magnificent nook. Being August, summer was almost over, but the happy plant was undergoing a second bloom and, while not as robust as the one from a few months ago, it was still an enchanting place to sit.

"What has happened?" The concern in Beth's pansy-blue eyes was touching. But she still had that smudge on her nose.

"You have dirt here." Diana reached out and brushed it off. "I went driving with Colonel Webster."

Beth nodded. "That sounds lovely. Where did you go?"

Diana took a deep, unsteady breath. "I barely remember, because I was so incensed that he treated Whinny and Whicker like *job horses*."

"Oh, dear." Beth pulled off her gardening gloves and put her hand over Diana's, which was clenched in her lap. "I suppose you said something?"

"How could I not, with poor Whinny all but stopped from the shock of being treated thus?"

She gasped. "And?"

"And I told him my opinion in no uncertain terms, but he deftly argued himself out of my bad books. Too deftly."

"That shows a superior intellect," Beth said dryly. "I can see why he is entering diplomatic service."

"And therein lay the problem," Diana said, pulling her hands from her friend's and wringing them. "I'm thinking thoughts."

Beth took a deep breath and let it out slowly. "Familiar, 'I don't want to marry this man,' thoughts?"

Thoughts that hinted she was not as engaged to Colonel Webster as the betrothal ring suggested. Diana blinked to stall the gathering tears. Angry, frustrated tears. *How did she end up here again?* "Yes, those kind. Although, this time I am not twenty-two, and I do not have my father to hold my hand and tell me I don't have to marry a man I cannot love, and that life will go on if I don't. Because he *wants* me to marry Colonel Webster." She drew in her own deep breath, which became part hiccup and part sob.

Beth put an arm around her, drawing her close. "All this from one drive? Come now, don't you think you should give this man —to whom, until now, you have been perfectly happily engaged —another chance? Perhaps you should get Pip to take him out to improve his skill with the ribbons. Perhaps he just hasn't handled such lovely horses?"

Diana searched Beth's face and saw the concern there. "You think I am rash? Oh, I know I am rash. But to think about using his whip on Whinny, and over such a trifle!"

"There can be no greater sin in your eyes than a man who mistreats a horse." Beth nodded. "But was this not the same man who you said used his last lot of army prize money to build a schoolhouse in his local village?"

Diana nodded and huffed, not wanting to think well of him.

"And did he not also tell you how he has an assortment of stray animals at his property, and hoped you would not mind too much?"

"He did. He probably whips them all."

Beth laughed. "He was probably nervous because he was driving one of the most notable female whips in the country. I think I can stand in for your mother for a moment and say that perhaps we should give him another chance."

It was no surprise that her friend took her fiancé's side in the matter. She had also cautioned against Diana breaking her engagement with Lord Fortescue. Indeed, Beth herself would never be so cavalier as to gamble with her own matrimony.

Diana sagged. "Oh, very well. But the moment I see him so much as growl at something ..."

"You will think about it then, and decide your best course of action. You do not want to act rashly, but you also do not want to spend the rest of your life with a man who mistreats God's creatures."

Diana took a deep breath. "Cordelia would never forgive me if I cry off. She takes full credit for this engagement and keeps bragging about Colonel Webster being the nephew of a duke. This is the first thing I've ever done that pleases her."

"She is quite high in the instep, isn't she?" Beth leaned in conspiratorially. "I overheard Mother telling Father the other day that Cordelia refused an invitation to the Healy's ball because she thought them a trifle common."

Diana had an image of Mrs. Healy, laughing good-naturedly when she read the refusal. Probably happy not to have Cordelia there, if truth be told. But it also meant Diana could not attend. And Cordelia had not even asked. "Oh no! I love the Healy's ball. Can I come with you? Although, wait a moment, when is it?"

"August fifteenth."

"That is the day before the race. And ..."

Beth's eyes were wide, and she shook her head slowly. "Diana, you *never would.*" Her voice was a mix of horror and awe.

Diana shrugged. "I am still thinking about it. Father has stupidly sold Equinox to the Prince of Wales, and I need funds to buy him back. I'm sure if I offer the prince more than he paid, he'll sell him back to me after the opening of his stables. Templeton said—"

Her friend looked up sharply. "Has he visited?"

Beth's wariness of Templeton grew from when Diana's last engagement had collapsed, and had never quite abated. She always maintained that it was Templeton who had lured Fortescue into talking inappropriately, and that he'd made sure it was done within Diana's earshot. But Beth gave Templeton too much credit for forethought, because the punch Templeton had given Fortescue was definitely not planned.

There was *no way* he would have done such a thing, letting her find out in such an unfortunate and embarrassing way. He just wouldn't.

"Yes. He stays with us and is mucking around in the stables with Pip. Too much of a bother to ride back and forth each day."

Beth raised her eyebrows. "That explains things. What is he encouraging you to do this time? Because I always know when you get into some kind of scrape, Templeton will not be far away."

"Not lately, though, you must admit." Diana stared into the distance, across the fence into the field beyond, where a herd of black-and-white cows cheerfully ate the late-blooming daisies that dotted it. Anything rather than feel sad for Templeton.

"Only because his father passed on, and he's had his hands too full with his inheritance."

"A fair point." She had missed him in those many months, though. Almost two years, in fact. And when he returned, he was swathed in shadow, even though he tried to be as teasing as ever. "No, he just questioned my engagement. Then told me the race is open to ladies if you read between the lines, and *et voila*, I am a seething mess of indecision."

"You *want* to drive in the race?" The incredulity in her friend's tone was hard to miss.

Diana turned sharply, eyebrows raised.

Beth closed her eyes for a moment, as though gathering her patience. "Of course you do. But Diana …"

Diana held up a hand. "I know." She could not bear to have her sins repeated back to her. But it didn't stop Beth, who took advantage of the fact they never minced words.

"You have only just rehabilitated your reputation from jilting Lord Fortescue. Everybody is convinced you've put that behind you. Why just last week, Lady Cummings was taking tea with Mother and said she was impressed with the way you have turned everything around."

"She likely didn't mention she was the first to turn her back on me."

Beth had the grace to blush. "Yes, I admit she did not. But Mother gently reminded her of how wrong she had been about you, and how right *you* had been about Lord Fortescue."

Diana smiled. Even when the worst had happened, Beth and her estimable family had stood by Diana and forced the rest of the village to do it too.

"You have just received and accepted an offer for a most eligible marriage, one mind you, that I am green with envy about.

Your future life will involve adventuring around the world in the most luxurious fashion. Why would you risk it? For what? Equinox deserves to be owned by the future king. He will live out his days treated like the prince he is."

Beth could never understand how much Equinox meant to her. She had not known him from his first shaky steps and fed him apples and sweeties every day hence. "He would think we abandoned him. He raced and won for us all those years, and I just want to race and win for him. As for being treated like a prince, that particular prince had to sell off his entire stud to the highest bidder just last year. How can I risk it? Equinox could end up anywhere! And Father would not have the funds to buy him back, because he's already spent all his blunt on new Arabian mares."

"If Colonel Webster is as against this as you say he is, you will make a fool of him. If you do it, you know what it will mean."

"That I may never get married?" Diana frowned. The risk was real.

Beth nodded, her mouth a flat frown. "That. But if you think your stepmama can't force your father to ship you off to your Aunt Victoria in Yorkshire, you underestimate her. You'll need the winnings from the race just to live."

"She would never ..." Diana thought about the myriad of ways Cordelia had changed their lives. How she could no longer chat to the maids, how the footmen now wore silver braided livery and had to speak in hushed tones, how they always ate in the formal dining room now, not to mention the endless needlework and pianoforte sessions. "You're right."

Beth regarded her sadly. "I don't want to tell you how many conversations Mother has had to endure with the new Mrs. Kingsley looking forward to your nuptials."

Diana shrugged. "It's not entirely her fault. I abhor her changes and she abhors me abhorring them." They laughed, and for the first time since Father told her he was selling Equinox, the sun peeked from behind the clouds.

Beth shrugged. "It would not have been easy to be the new Mrs. Kingsley with the formidable Miss Kingsley already ruling the roost."

Diana exhaled. "And thus we find ourselves here." It certainly seemed like there might be repercussions she hadn't thought of. Cordelia sent any servant who didn't act with perfect propriety packing, without a reference. It was entirely possible she would do the same to a stepdaughter.

Then Beth jumped up from the garden seat. "What if you help Pip race and buy Equinox with his winnings if he comes first? Surely it doesn't matter which Kingsley races as long as one of you wins?"

Diana smiled at Beth's excitement. "That's what I said. He is definitely entering, and I will do my utmost to help him. But ..."

"Don't you dare say you are a better whip!"

"I would never dare." Beth would not hear of anyone being better at anything than Pip. It had been so since they were both about fifteen.

"What *would* you do to help him? Nothing illicit, I hope."

Diana feigned injury, putting a hand over her heart. "I don't need to be illicit, oh ye of little faith. He will have to get Father's consent, of course, but I would like to have all our own horses and grooms at each of the changes so we might change them in under two minutes."

Beth clapped. "That's *brilliant.*"

"Well, I was thinking of it for myself, but I should listen to you, my dear friend." For once, she really should listen to the voice of reason. Equinox would be fine with the Prince of Wales. And he had Honey, the love of his life, with him. She would miss him more than he would miss her. It was time to put these rash thoughts behind her once and for all and make a decision for her own future.

Beth nodded. "Yes, you should. Will you still go to Brighton?" She smoothed her skirts, inspecting them closely. It would be Beth's heart's desire to attend anything at the Prince of Wales's seaside home. Especially if Pip was there.

"I am invited to the opening, but not the ball. We will probably stay at Uncle Horatio's since he will be in London. Perhaps we can convince your mother to let you come with us? We may get a last-minute invite to the ball, too, although I'm sure it will be a sad squeeze."

It was not an outrageous request. Beth had traveled to Brighton with the Kingsley family many summers and knew Uncle Horatio almost as well as Diana did herself.

"May I? Truly? Perhaps we can stop at one of the stage changes along the way and cheer the gentlemen on."

"Excellent idea," Diana agreed. "Let's ask your parents. I shall put on my best manners and say nothing about the fact that I dearly wanted to race myself."

"Not unless you want a hearty lecture from my mother," Beth replied. "Goodness, what am I going to wear? There is no time for anything new!"

"There's that new silk dress your mother is making, and I'm sure I can persuade Papa to allow us to visit the haberdasher in Brighton for some new gloves."

"Oh, I could never …" Beth said, but there was a sparkle in her eye.

"You know better than to deny me the pleasure of buying you things. After all, you've just saved my future marriage."

Beth shrugged. "When you phrase it that way …"

They stood and took the winding path to the front door.

"I am glad you came to speak to me," Beth said. "We have averted a disaster."

"You told me what I needed to hear," Diana said. "Even if it wasn't what I wanted to hear."

Diana followed Beth inside the vicarage. So why did it feel like nothing they had agreed to would stick? Like the moment she mounted Equinox, her resolution to marry Colonel Webster and not race to Brighton would fly from her head with the late afternoon breeze?

CHAPTER 8

WHERE BACON LOSES ITS APPEAL

In the end, Alec had skipped dinner *en famille*. The thought of listening to Colonel Webster and Diana talk about wedding dates and plans was too much for his stomach to bear. They had sent up a tray, which he demolished, and then he read by candlelight and put himself to bed, imagining the way Diana would look at Colonel Webster and put her hand over his at the dining room table.

So, not the best of evenings. But he had no one but himself to blame.

He woke up just after five and went to the library to work on his own race plan. Diana would probably forget she'd promised to help him. He was on his own. Heaven knew what she had planned for Pip, but with the entire Kingsley fortune at her disposal, it was likely impressive.

After two hours, his stomach groaned and grumbled like an old man getting out of a chair. Breakfast was needed, and at this hour, Diana would likely still be abed. He would wander down to the dining room and find something to eat, and perhaps even ferret some fruit for the little bag he'd been collecting for when he left them. Which would be soon. He wouldn't stay much longer.

He had eaten better food in the past five days than he had the entire month before. The breeches that had been woefully loose upon his arrival were once again snug, and he felt more like himself and a little less desperate.

The Kingsleys would never know how grateful he was to them.

He ordered bacon, poached eggs, and toast. Far too much, really, but he couldn't help himself.

The footman poured him a cup of delicious-smelling coffee. He turned. "Thank you, my good man," he said, adding cream and sugar to just the right consistency. The toast came first, so he spread it thick with marmalade. They made the best marmalade at Kingsley. Perhaps he could convince Cook to part with a jar of it when he left?

His meal arrived and he was halfway through when Diana entered with Colonel Webster. He sighed in resignation and stood, as they came to the table. "Good morning."

She dipped a curtsey. "Good morning, Lord Templeton." She was wearing a white muslin gown covered in sprigs of green and trimmed with green velvet ribbon. *Lovely.*

She sat next to her fiancé and they ordered breakfast, which for the Colonel was egg, bacon, and a side plate of kippers. *May they give you fish breath, my friend.*

Alec had to be careful here. It was all very well for him to contrive to break up one bad engagement, when Lord Fortescue was a scoundrel, but was Colonel Webster one too? If she was marrying a perfectly fine gentleman, he would have to step back and allow her to do it. All he knew was what Pip had told him— that he was the nephew of the Duke of Wellsmore. So, he'd best get to know the man a little more.

"A lovely morning, is it not?" he said jovially. "I trust you slept well. I find the beds here in Kingsley House an absolute treat."

Colonel Webster had a friendly smile on his face. "I had the best sleep I have had since I was a babe, I'm sure of it."

Damnation, he was personable. Nothing high in the instep about him, duke's nephew or not.

He could not help but notice Webster had a fair smattering of silver at his temples and more than a few lines around his eyes. Not that there was anything wrong with silver hair or wrinkles, but it felt like Diana was marrying a man only a little younger than her father. He probably became a colonel when Diana was still climbing trees.

"I hear you are a friend of Mr. Kingsley," Alec said, fishing. He knew no such thing, but it would make perfect sense to him if Colonel Webster somehow knew Diana's father.

"Why, yes. We are members of the same clubs, of course, but we also attended Eton within a few years of each other."

Aha! He was *much* too old for Diana. He stopped his gloating when he saw Diana glaring at him, as though she had divined his purpose exactly. Alec forged on. "You probably knew my father, too," he said, careful to hide his glee.

He nodded and smiled sadly, as though sending Alec condolences. "Indeed, I did, although he was a few years older again than Diana's father, but his reputation lingered."

That Alec could well believe. His father had lived the high life right from the very beginning, as had his father before him.

"What did they call him? Toady Templeton?" Colonel Webster laughed. "I'm sure you are nothing like him."

Alec stilled. Was Webster roasting him or trying to make him look bad in front of Diana? His manners and smoothness made it impossible to tell. But his father *had* been called Toady Templeton because he would do anything, give anything, to keep up with the Prince of Wales.

Everybody thought Alec was cut from the same cloth because he resembled his father so closely in looks. Nothing could be further from the truth, although circumstances probably intervened before he could travel down that path.

Still, it would never do for anyone in society to think that their fortunes had been reversed so harshly. He spent most of his time paddling as hard as he could, trying to make it all look effortless and like nothing had changed in his earldom. "Yes, my father was quite a unique creature."

Somehow the conversation had gone from Alec interrogating Colonel Webster to Webster finding the one thing that could embarrass Alec more than anything else and turning his thumb on it. He looked at the man with a new sense of admiration. He certainly knew how to flip a conversation and be thoroughly nice about it. But then he *was* a diplomat.

"I hear you have joined the diplomatic corps," Alec said. "Where is your first posting?"

"I was lucky enough to be required in Calcutta." He turned to Diana and put his hand over hers. "And I will have a delightful wife by my side."

Alec couldn't seem to take his eyes from the large hand placed over Diana's, like a nightmare come true. Obviously, skipping dinner wasn't going far enough.

Before he could pull his eyes away, she had deftly pulled her hand out and made an act of taking a sip of her chocolate.

Alec nodded. "From all accounts it is a wonderful place to visit." He left the rest of the thought unsaid—that while it would be a lovely place to visit, it would be an uncomfortably hot place to *live*.

Mr. and Mrs. Kingsley joined them at the table, one sitting next to Alec and the other next to Diana. "Good morning, all."

Before he could reply, Diana changed the topic of conversation. "Good morning. Father, I was looking at my trousseau, and there is much I need to add to it. Could you take me to London in a few weeks?"

Mr. Kingsley looked at his daughter and shook his head. "I'm sorry, my dear, but I will be in Brighton, making sure Equinox is settling in. But perhaps your brother might take you? He will go to London for the start of the race, after all. You can take the carriage to Brighton once you have done your shopping."

Alec laughed to himself. How nimbly she just transported herself to London to watch the start of the race.

"Your fiancé might have something to say in these proceedings," Cordelia said. "Colonel Webster, would you prefer to escort Diana and Pip?"

He shook his head. "No, I thank you. I must visit my uncle. He would like me to represent his business interests in India."

Diana smiled brightly. "And the shopping will be most tedious. Not nearly as important as a duke's summons!"

But Cordelia frowned. "Very well." She turned to Diana. "You can take Mariah with you."

Diana paused. "Could Beth come with me instead? She loves Brighton and would be a much better companion for me."

Mrs. Kingsley nodded in agreement. "That is the perfect solution. Pip can take you both. He will be there for his race, and you can do your shopping and then go onward to Brighton where you will meet up with us. Tell Mrs. Cartwright that I will send two grooms to attend you." She frowned, obviously thinking. "And an outrider."

Remembering the conversation yesterday in the library, he believed Diana had planned this entire conversation from beginning to end to get exactly what she wanted. And if he was not mistaken, what she wanted was not shopping on Bond Street, but to watch the race itself from somewhere on the Brighton Road so she could support Pip. Or maybe even *race* herself.

And then, of course, there was the school of thought that if Diana was so adept at getting what she wanted, she must actually *want* to marry Colonel Webster, which was sobering.

He had not finished the fine piece of bacon on his plate, but he rose from the table, regardless. There was only so much time a man could spend sitting with a newly engaged couple.

"Thank you for a lovely breakfast. I look forward to seeing you in London, Miss Kingsley, and hope you will grant me some token of good luck before the race."

He didn't wait for a response, just bowed and sauntered from the room like he hadn't a care in the world. He imagined Diana wistfully watching him leave, admiring his graceful form.

He didn't look back, because it would not be true.

CHAPTER 9

WHERE ALEC GETS A LESSON IN DRIVING TO AN INCH

Two weeks later, Alec was ensconced in a leather chair at Brooks. The steak was good, but was this place worth the ten pounds membership? Or would it be noticed and commented on if he let it lapse? His membership to Watier's was cancelled when he refused to meet the minimum amount they expected one to gamble. Call him mad, but a minimum of twenty pounds a week was insane.

Alec was handed a note by a server. The man hovered with his silver tray in hand. "A reply was requested, my lord."

Alec raised an eyebrow in question and unfolded the small piece of parchment to find Diana's loopy scrawl.

T,

Come driving with me. I await you out front.

Ever your faithful huntress,

Miss Kingsley

He broke out in a grin. Seeing her scrawling penmanship made his heart lighter. He folded the newspaper, collected his coat and hat, and sauntered outside, where Miss Diana Kingsley sat atop a shiny red perch phaeton.

The white feathers on her bonnet blew in the breeze and the

look she threw at him was entirely rebellious. His heart stuttered and came to a complete stop. *How lovely you are.*

He schooled his expression into indifference. "No need to look at *me* like that, my dear. I am the last person to admonish you for driving down St. James Street with little more than a bonnet for chaperone."

She smiled in answer and patted the seat next to her.

After he climbed onto the tight little seat that was mostly taken up by her scarlet military-style driving ensemble, she threw the young man at the horses' heads a coin, which he caught deftly. "My thanks!"

Alec looked up at the skies. It was not the perfect morning for a drive in Hyde Park. The season was turning and there were as many cool days now as there were warm. But when Miss Kingsley drove to your club and requested your presence, no sane man refused, if only to discover what on earth she was scheming.

Fog crept through the city, clinging to the buildings like a foul mood, but Diana pulled her tan kid gloves on in a businesslike way and eyed the sky with nothing of the trepidation Alec felt.

"Perhaps we could have saved this for tomorrow," he said, as droplets of cold London rain sprinkled his face. "Or better yet, a closed carriage might be the go."

Diana smiled brightly at him, as though he had just told a grand joke. Before she set off, she checked the rig with her expert eye. Then she threaded the reins through her fingers with a deftness that never failed to impress him.

"Are you worried about my hat?" She patted the back of the confection that was more feather than bonnet. "I assure you it's the oldest I have and due for replacement."

"Actually, I was more concerned with us getting soaked to the skin. It seems like years since you've taken me driving, and I own I want to enjoy it."

She took off with a gentle nudge of her team and glided into the traffic like the accomplished whip she was.

"I see you still drive to an inch. I do miss seeing you tool around Hyde Park in that high-perch phaeton you used to have. Golden days."

Diana would have none of his wistfulness, raising her chin and setting her gaze straight ahead. "Father sold it." Her words were clipped and while there was no emotion in them, Alec knew how much the sale of it and the beautiful, highly-sprung team she had drawing it must have cost her.

"And you stopped coming to London in any case. I always thought you were the kind to ride out a storm." He raised his eyes to the darkening clouds above, as if to prove a point. He thought no such thing, of course. No lady could outrun the outrage that followed her jilting of Fortescue. But he wanted her to share how it affected her, all the same. He had set the wheels in motion of the jilting. But never in his wildest dreams did he imagine her doing what she did.

To this day, he could take himself back to St. George's Hanover Square, the congregation made up of the cream of London society. There were more titles in that church than you'd find in a circulating library.

He'd been incredibly saddened she was going through with the marriage, first of all. And that feeling fought strongly with the urge to walk down the aisle and plant the groom a facer. Not only was he only entering the marriage for Diana's dowry, which comprised piles of money and Equinox at the height of his power, but the scoundrel had no intention of ever loving her. If she was going to marry a man who needed her money, she might as well have married him.

Not that he expected Equinox to go down the aisle in her place. He'd not seen that coming.

It really was more than fair that she stayed away from London when at all possible, because whenever she went, whispers followed, snickering began.

"Beyond my control, Templeton. When I sent Equinox down the aisle for me, I envisaged my own ruin at Society's hand, but not my father's. In London, he couldn't even take Walnut for a walk without somebody giving him the cut direct."

Walnut was the family spaniel, with doleful eyes and a penchant for chewing boots. He shrugged. "Society is a harsh mistress."

She rolled her eyes. "This from society's darling, who has never incurred its wrath."

"Oh, yes, that's me. Can't put a foot wrong." Little did she know the frantic paddling to keep society at bay.

She kept her eyes firmly on the road ahead. "Or, if you put a foot wrong, suddenly all the young pups are walking down Bond Street with their boots on backwards because you've started a fashion. Like those ridiculous daffodils you took to wearing in your buttonhole."

The mist turned to drizzle. He reached behind to pull the hood of the phaeton forward a little farther. "I may not be so fashionable after the ball in Brighton."

"Do tell? I don't have an invitation." Just the thought of him doing something that would get him in trouble seemed to perk her up. She took the corner with astounding precision.

"No, I don't think I will tell," he said, just to annoy her.

"Oh, but now I *must* be there to see it, for I cannot be kept in suspense."

"How do you intend to do that without an invitation?"

She arched an eyebrow. "Surely yours includes a partner?"

"Alas, it does not." Although, if it did, he would love to have her on *his* arm instead of Webster's.

They approached the gates of Hyde Park, but it was too early for any kind of traffic to hold her up. She sailed through and down Rotton Row. "Will you dance with me at the ball?"

"The ball you are not coming to?" How long would it take her to come to the point? She obviously wanted something, because he could count on zero fingers the amount of times she had sought his company without that of her brother. But he could happily sit next to her, admiring her complete mastery of her high-strung team. "You really are the most complete hand."

She turned to him, her golden-brown eyes lighting with pleasure. "How lovely of you to say so. I do think, from one whip to another, that you have a very good chance of winning. You have already done Brighton in under six hours, have you not?"

He nodded. "I have."

"I know you are aware of what Pip is doing with his winnings."

Ah. There it was. She wanted his winnings. He almost laughed at the thought of giving the very rich Miss Kingsley money.

"It's just a lark for him," she continued. "He has no need of the prize money."

This implied that neither did he.

That was the funny thing about rich people. They had no concept of what things cost. And equally no concept that others might be in a distinctly different situation. He remembered being the same way himself for all of his years, bar the last two.

"If I should be so lucky as to win, the purse is already well and truly accounted for," he said easily.

She frowned, and he imagined the cogs of her mind spinning, trying to find the quickest route to getting what she wanted. He'd like her less if she wasn't doing that.

"Don't you want to know what Pip is giving it to me for?"

He took a deep breath of damp park air, which was a mix of wet grass and damp gravel. "I was there, remember? You aim to buy Equinox back from the Prince. As if he'd let him go."

She huffed. "He might!"

Unfortunately she had forgotten one thing. "But if I win,

certainly you know I will attempt to obtain Equinox for my own." He *would* make a wonderful partner for Penelope.

Keeping a steady hand on her reins, she darted him a furious side glance. "You would keep him away from his home?" Her mouth settled into a frown. "I think less of you."

He shrugged at her outraged profile. "Of course you do. I'm not doing your bidding. That always annoys you." She really should have been a duchess. Her long patrician nose in the air and her eyes sparkling with anger. At him. The nephew of a duke was just a waste.

She tossed her head back. "I don't know why I bothered talking to you, much less helping you with your race. I get nothing in return."

"Now, now, we never help others to be helped ourselves, but out of the goodness in our hearts." With each word he was making her angrier. But damned if he was going to hand over either the prize money or the horse it might buy. "And I am very grateful for the suggestion to buy Equinox, I had not thought of it. Although the temptation to go shopping for new boots is cursed strong."

Her hands briefly clenched the reins before she controlled herself. "Ooh, you are infuriating! If only I could enter the race myself."

"Although I first suggested it, I admit to being grateful you are not. You'd be in Brighton before my team had worn out their starting jitters."

Instead of amusing her, his comment seemed to deflate her, and her anger dissipated. She turned to him and smiled, her eyes sad. "I would love nothing more." She smiled ruefully. "So, obviously I cannot."

Intriguing. "How is it obvious?"

She stared ahead, her jaw set. "Because my impulses are not to be trusted, dear Templeton. I am well acquainted with them. Beth put me to rights, and I have not wavered since."

Sadness, too, and it had nothing to do with the fact that the drizzle was strengthening into something one could call rain. "I prefer to think that some of your best decisions have been your most impetuous ones."

She had put herself in a box, much like that fateful time she'd locked herself in a chest while playing hide-and-seek when they were children. Except that this time, even though he could hear her cries, just as he had back then, there was no way he could unlock it for her. This time she was in a box of her own making, and there was nothing for it. Her reputation was now made of the sheerest gossamer, easy to rend and impossibly fragile.

"Well, I for one would like to see their faces if you trotted up to the pavilion, cheeks flushed, hat blown away, in first place," he said. "I would be entirely proud." It was the kind of image that would keep him awake at night.

She took a breath so deep her shoulders shrugged with it. "Indeed, you could afford to be proud, because the aftereffect would have no bearing on you. But can you imagine? Colonel Webster would end up just like Lord Fortescue and be the butt of every joke for months if not years to come."

"Fortescue deserved it." His voice was so quiet, he wouldn't be surprised if she hadn't heard him.

But she had. "I agree. But did Father deserve what came afterward?"

"Is accepting Webster's hand in marriage part of your redemption?"

She thought about it, eased the horses as they rounded a slight bend, and nodded slowly.

He found he quite liked not driving, even if it was raining. It gave him more time to concentrate on Diana, rather than what his horses were about to do.

"I cannot help feeling that the chapter will only be properly closed upon my marriage." Alec didn't say anything, not trusting himself, but she must have read his expression. "He's a good man.

The only man interested, if you must know. I suppose he's been out of the country so long he missed all the outrage."

He felt his eyes widen with shock and worked hard to relax his face into mild appreciation of her joke. True, he had been withdrawn from society since the death of his father and the deluge of problems that came with it, but he should have been there to help her through this. She might be headstrong, but by God, her spirit was brighter than the sun. Any man could see she was a woman beyond compare. How could Webster be the only man?

He should have pursued her, taken her to wife despite her father's disapproval and his own poor state. Or better yet, done it when he was one-and-twenty, his father was still alive, and Alec didn't know about the future mountain of debt he was to inherit. Grief swirled in his stomach at the thought that he hadn't tried harder or approached her directly when he could have. When he should have.

What would he have to look forward to if it wasn't bantering with her or seeing the light shine in her eyes when she made a direct hit on him?

His best friend's sister.

Was there anything more clichéd?

They drove in silence for a few moments more until the drizzle became so strong that the bonnet wasn't doing its job. He reached behind him and wrestled it forward to shield them from the worst of the rain.

"Why thank you. That's very thoughtful."

Rain dripped down the side of the hood and onto the arm of his coat, which now smelled like a wet sheep. "It would have been more thoughtful of me to refuse the drive and have a nice hot cup of tea with you by the fireside in the library instead."

"Did you know you have not wished me happy?"

Of course he hadn't. "I always wish you happy. Surely you know that?"

She smiled at him and so help him, the clouds parted a little, and the rain slowed. Or seemed to.

He had scuttled her last engagement and had thankfully succeeded. But Fortescue was so obviously a bad match that he felt vindicated in saving her from it, never dreaming she would jilt Fortescue the way she did, or that it would have such lasting repercussions.

Was he encouraging her to enter the race and behave scandalously so that this engagement, too, would fail? That if two engagements fell apart, Beau Kingsley would finally look at the man still standing by her side and give him permission to court her, impoverished or not?

But that wasn't being fair to her. If she wanted to marry, she had every right to do so, and he was a monster to try to stop it. He either had to tell her how he felt and let the chips fall where they may, or he had to bow out gracefully and support her as the brother she thought him to be.

What a damnable mess.

"Diana, I must apologize to you."

She turned to him, surprise written in the *O* her mouth formed. "Do go on."

He took a deep breath. "I have encouraged you to enter the race, and I should not have. In truth, nothing could be worse for your reputation, nothing more injurious to your family. It was wrong of me. One would hope I had grown sufficiently to know what is expected and required of a young lady embarking upon her marriage. It seems I still think you are a fourteen-year-old who is up for all manner of larks." He shook his head ruefully. "In conclusion, I'm sorry. I can see it causes you grief, on occasion, to be constricted by the bounds our society puts on us. The last thing I want to do is add to that grief."

He turned to look at her, only to see tears pooling in her eyes that meant he had yet again added to her sadness. He wanted to place his hand on her hers, say something consoling, but he knew better. She would hate him for it.

Congratulations, Alec my boy. You've once again made things worse just by opening your mouth.

"Pish posh, Templeton. As though anything you could say would make me downcast. I'm lucky. I have Pip, who is such a capital whip, to do what I would dearly love to do myself. Perhaps better than I would do myself."

"Now, now, my dear. Doing it too brown. We both know that's not true."

"Yes, well, that's all you're going to get from me on the subject. I am happy. You need to wish me happy. That is all."

He turned and met her martial gaze. She was an impenetrable wall he had no hope or right to scale. She didn't want to hear his soppy declarations of love at this point. He had lost this race. She was gone. "I wish you happy."

With all his heart he wished her happy.

CHAPTER 10

THE WHITE HORSE HOTEL—PICCADILLY STREET, LONDON

The courtyard in front of the White Horse Hotel, on the corner of Piccadilly and Dover Streets, was a throng of carriages, dogs, spectators, and entrants—and everyone was yelling.

The smell of leather rode the air, along with the sound of horses stomping and tackle jingling. Indeed, if a mill broke out, or a horse bolted in the excitement, he would not be surprised. The newspapers had done their job, ensuring half of London was at the starting line.

There was even conjecture the prince was going to race himself to defend his four-and-a-half-hour record to Brighton.

Unlikely.

Alec sat in his curricle, sixth down in a line of eleven entrants, each with a red ribbon threaded through the wheel spokes to identify them. He did some calculating. Eleven entries multiplied by one hundred was over a thousand guineas prize money. A fortune. A life-changing fortune.

Alec took a swig from his flask of lukewarm coffee, which did nothing to help his jitters. In fact, it seemed only to make them worse. He flexed his hands, then shook them out, looking up at the cloudy London sky for some calm.

Perhaps it was just that the prince's friends were standing in a loud, foolish group nearby. So many of them were cronies of his father's. The same people, coincidentally, who led his father deeper into debt, trying to keep up with their fast lifestyle.

He should hate them, but they were probably just as deep in debt as his father had been, as he now was. They huddled in a group, inspecting the entrants' equipages and, if Alec wasn't mistaken, placing last-minute bets in a swift flurry of paper swapping.

People had pushed back the curtains of the red brick hotel and now hung from every window. A group of ladies on the first floor waved scarfs from their balcony.

"Good morning, Lord Templeton," one shouted. "I wish you luck!" The others laughed as she blushed.

He waved back. "Good morning, ladies."

The marshal stood atop a box at the front of the entrant line. He was a mutton-chopped man, with a bright red nose that raised questions about his sobriety. How the entrants were going to hear him above this din was anyone's guess.

He cleared his throat. "Attention racers and distinguished guests."

The crowd hushed a degree. The marshal bowed toward the group of Prinny's cronies and then turned to address the line of racing curricles and their drivers.

"We will begin the time trial in fifteen minutes. Contestants will take the Sutton-Reigate route to Brighton and must check into each predetermined stage before reaching the marine pavilion in Brighton. Each curricle is allowed two contestants and either may drive. I will release you in fifteen-minute incre-ments to make your way to Brighton at your leisure."

There was appreciative laughter from the crowd at the

thought of the race being leisurely. It was going to be a race to hell in a handbasket if he had any precognition at all. But the "two contestants" rule was new to him. Diana would most assuredly have raced with her brother if she had but known it.

"One of Mr. Vulliamy's associates will be at each stage to record your arrival and obtain your signature."

Mr. Vulliamy himself, the master clockmaker, stepped forward and bowed. Alec recognized him from a visit with his father to a Pall Mall shop five years ago. He had purchased an ormolu clock for the prince's birthday that had a small porcelain statue of a beautiful lady leaning on an urn. He had found the bill for it after his father's death—unpaid. He had made sure the clockmaker received his money, for it seemed grossly unfair that something so beautiful should be considered free.

Mr. Vulliamy looked around at the mayhem with a sharp eye and an amused expression, like a man who was going to enjoy his part in the proceedings. "We will tabulate the times, and announce the winner at the ball tomorrow evening."

Everything sounded eminently fair, so what made him suspicious? He couldn't shake that feeling, no more than he could shake the nerves lingering in his stomach. Perhaps it was just impossible to believe that it could be fair with such a vast amount of money at stake.

The marshal spoke again. "The Prince of Wales would like to announce that he will match your entry purses." There was a roar of approval from the crowd. "With this grand prize in mind, I urge you to consider the safety of your fellow travelers at all times." The crowd laughed as though that were an even bigger joke. He frowned and continued. "And to keep to the rules of fair play."

A male voice from the front of the line said, "There was nothing in the race rules at White's about fair play. Indeed, I believe it said 'fair means or foul.'"

Now the crowd truly broke into laughter. But Alec's stomach tightened. He didn't remember seeing that. Thank goodness Diana had decided not to enter.

"Whoever actually *makes* it to Brighton gets the prize," said someone in the prince's group. "Then he'll hang for the crimes he committed to get there!"

"Lay you odds it's Lady Archer," another voice yelled out, but the crowd was too busy for Alec to make out who.

Alec craned his neck around to look behind him. A lady, dressed in white muslin and a white bonnet and no driving coat to speak of, raised her whip, accepting the riotous cheering directed at her. *So, there was a lady entrant.* Diana would be furious. Speaking of Diana …

He scanned the crowd, looking for her. She had to be somewhere. There was no way she'd let Pip start the race by himself. Pip was behind him, but he had nobody with him apart from his groom.

Surely she would be there to wish him luck? He sat back, deflated, and took another swig of coffee. Her circumstances had changed now. She was to be a married lady and couldn't go scampering about as she once had.

He pulled out his gold pocket watch, which he'd inherited from his father and would one day pass to his son. It was another Vulliamy masterpiece of brilliant blue enamel and inlaid gold. It was ten minutes until race time. He snapped it shut and put it in the pocket of his greatcoat.

Noted Corinthian, Captain Malmsbury, had drawn the coveted first place and would leave at seven o'clock. He would have the cleanest ride, with less traffic and no racers ahead of him. Those leaving later would have to contend with all manner of wagons, stagecoaches, and carriages that took the Brighton Road daily.

The captain was out of his curricle and walking up and down

the line of contestants that stretched two blocks down Piccadilly Street. He reminded Alec of a rooster, with his chest puffed out so far it arrived five minutes ahead of him. He might be first in the race, but nobody expected him to win because he was a famously reckless driver.

He stopped beside Alec. "Beautiful day for a ride, eh, Templeton?" Being a member of the Four Horse Club, he was wearing a blue waistcoat with inch-thick yellow stripes and long drab coat with mother-of-pearl buttons. "I consider my luck well and truly set, having drawn first out of the gate. Can't see me losing from there."

If you can manage not to crash into anything. He knew the captain well enough to know that he didn't like him. He was brash and entirely too full of himself. But he and Malmsbury were members of the same secret club—Wrack and Ruin, especially set up by Viscount Beaufort for gentlemen who had inherited debt through no fault of their own.

They shared opportunities and knowledge, whether it be tips for the 'Change or the latest agricultural method to get more out of their land. The only rule was that gambling was forbidden, since, for the most part, it was what got their families into trouble to start with. So, they tolerated Malmsbury, for he had suffered just as they had.

"I'm sure you will have a wonderful ride, Malmsbury. You're a capital whip, and it will be up to the rest of us to beat you." Actually, Alec felt quietly confident that both he and Pip could knock Malmsbury off his perch.

A young boy, who looked no more than six but was probably twelve, wove his way through the racegoers, stopping next to Alec. He held up his cap. "A penny, sir, a penny, and luck will be with you."

Alec fished into his coin bag and threw a few shillings into the open cap. "Let's see what that buys me!"

The shillings were pocketed in a flash, and the boy grinned. "Probably not a lot."

"Out of the way, boy," Malmsbury said, then looked over his shoulder at Alec. "Things are dire when you need luck from street urchins."

"I take what I can get," Alec replied with a shrug.

Malmsbury laughed and continued down the line of entrants, shaking hands with grooms and gentlemen alike and acting like he owned the race.

How much money had been placed on him for the win? How many people would lose hundreds or perhaps thousands of pounds if he lost? White's had been a madhouse, with people placing bets in their books. He'd even heard that the bookmakers who frequented Newmarket had set up odds on each racer. Considerable money was being shifted around the Beau Monde for this race.

And then, before he had a chance to ready his horses, the steward announced one minute to race time, and the crowd pushed them-selves back onto the footpath, shouting and waving handkerchiefs and flags above their heads. It was such a hullabaloo that Alec could barely hear it when the race began, and Captain Malmsbury took off with a loud "rar" that only whipped the crowd into a bigger uproar.

He was looking at the four curricles still ahead of him when he noticed the harness on his left-wheeler horse flapped with the horse's jostling. Alarm ran through him. He turned to his groom. "Stephen, can you please check the tack again?"

The groom jumped down. "A third time?"

"Indulge me," he said lazily.

Stephen's eyes flared. All his staff knew the more laid-back Alec sounded, the more dire the situation was.

Sure enough, a few moments later Alec heard Stephen's soft oath. The groom looked up, fury in his eyes. "It's been cut down low. I swear it wasn't like that five minutes ago."

Alec swore under his breath. There were so many people milling around, and it might even have been an urchin with a very sharp knife and a new coin in his pocket for the job. He just hoped it wasn't the one he'd just given three shillings to.

Having the harness cut like that would mean that once out on the open road, it would slip and slide, making controlling the horse more difficult and possibly causing an accident. His stomach churned as the nerves kicked harder. Whoever did this was not playing nice.

He turned back to Pip. "Check your rig, and tell everyone behind you to check theirs. Part of my harness has been cut."

A few moments later, everyone had checked, and all seemed in order. Except for Alec, that was. "Stephen, pull out the spares kit."

The emergency kit had buckles and lengths of leather that could be cut to any length in case of breakage. Most carriages had them, but if he'd only discovered this issue while they were driving at a fast pace, the curricle could've crashed. Precious time would be lost, the race along with it. Or his life. Or Stephen's. It was no small matter.

If this was what happened before the race began, what was in store for them along the road? No prize was worth a carriage accident. He had too many people depending on him.

"Be careful, Pip," he yelled out behind him. "I have a bad feeling about this."

"Oh, you old woman, it's going to be fine!" Pip replied, laughter in his voice. "Don't let a little loose strap spook you. This race is ours to win, and if I don't win it, or you don't win it, Diana is going to kill us. Think of that. It will make you race faster."

The thought of Diana at the finish line was certainly enough to race for. Especially when he imagined her being overcome with gratitude when he won and bought her horse from the prince for his stables. And a diabolic plan formed in his head. If he did manage to win, how much did Diana love her horse? Enough to throw over an engagement and marry him?

Something to race for indeed.

CHAPTER 11

IN WHICH DIANA MAY AS WELL HAVE RAISED
HER SWORD AND YELLED, "CHALLENGE
ACCEPTED."

In Sutton, thirteen miles south of London, the morning of the race dawned clear and crisp, with a chill in the air like the promise of autumn to come.

Nerves assailed Diana as soon as she opened her eyes. Although, how she could have been any more organized was impossible to say.

She and Beth were at the first stage, having been escorted there by Father and Cordelia the previous day on their way to Brighton. It had taken some time to convince them to allow them to stay the night at The Cock Hotel, and only the escort of her maid and the two grooms that were already there to help with the change convinced them.

It helped that her family stayed at The Cock often on their way to Brighton, and Father considered himself fast friends with the owner, Gentleman Jackson. The boxer had been mounted on many Kingsley horses over the years. Indeed, there was a very special bottle of brandy in the taproom with Beau Kingsley's name written across the label in ink.

Diana pulled back the curtain and squinted through the window. Peered actually, because the glass was square-cut, likely installed in the time of Henry the Eighth and possibly not cleaned since then.

Mariah, Diana's maid, helped her dress quietly, but Beth stirred anyway. She sat sleepily and yawned, her bed cap crooked and her wild dark curls escaping out of it. "Oh, must we get up already?"

"The race started an hour ago. I don't want to miss anything."

Sutton was less than two hours from London at the pace the drivers would take, although because they staggered the start, they would not expect to see Pip or Alec for some time after that.

"Templeton was to leave at a quarter past eight, was he not?"

Nerves squirmed in her stomach. Much as Templeton had annoyed her by not agreeing to buy Equinox for her, she couldn't deny that his new breeding program would be greatly bolstered by having him in his stable. It was hard not to want to wish him to win, even if it meant beating Pip. Assuming that the prince would sell him at all.

"Yes, and Pip at quarter to nine." It was the luck of the draw, and although it would have been better had they left earlier, there was nothing for it. They would bear the brunt of the daily traffic of wagons and carriages that frequented the Brighton Road. "We can't miss them, dearest. I will go downstairs and bespeak us some breakfast and a strong pot of coffee."

"Chocolate for me, please," said Beth, "and perhaps some bread and butter."

Diana curtsied. "Yes, ma'am. I shall also check on the grooms and make sure everything is ready. I will change those horses myself if I have to, but I own I would rather not."

She had promised Cordelia she would be on her best behavior, and she was sure that did not include changing horses in the courtyard of a public inn.

Diana made her way downstairs, the old treads creaking merrily with each step, and completed all of her tasks. She was waiting in the front room with a table laid with a crisp white tablecloth and some fruit buns and bread when Beth surfaced a half hour later.

"I suppose I must eat one of those fruit buns to keep up my strength," Beth said with a twinkle in her eye. She took a slab of butter and spread it over the bun, sighing in contentment.

Diana felt too nervous to eat, but the bread was crusty and the cheese just the right kind of sharp that soon she sighed just as happily as Beth.

Before long, they heard shouts from the courtyard, and a quick peek outside showed it was ablaze with excitement, ostlers and grooms running across the small space in a panic.

The first entrant had arrived and, to make matters worse, a coach had also arrived from London at the same time. The occupants of the coach were spilling into the courtyard, impeding the grooms and ostlers. One man demanded to know what the devil was going on and "where is my breakfast?"

In the middle of the uproar, a young man stood with a large notebook in his right hand and had a watch at the ready in his left.

"This is so entertaining," Diana said. "Do come and look. I don't know who that man is in the undertaker's garb, but I have never seen someone so nervous around a horse. Why is he standing in the middle of the courtyard? What is he doing?"

Beth poked her head over Diana's shoulder. "That will be the clockmaker's representative. I read in the newspaper that Vulliamy sent one to each change to make sure the entire race was chronicled."

Diana pursed her mouth. "Interesting. Because from everything Pip says, people are assuming this race is ripe for foul play. But I suppose at least the times will be correct."

Her friend pulled back and Diana read the shock on her face. "Oh, no, I'm sure you're mistaken. The prince would not put his name to such a thing."

"I'm sure you're right," Diana replied, smiling at Beth,

although there was every possibility the prince was oblivious or just thought the entire race was a bit of fun.

A curricle had a red ribbon threaded through the wheel spokes. It was splashed with mud but its yellow paint still gleamed in the sunshine.

The timekeeper stepped forward after the vehicle had halted. "Your name, sir."

The driver swept off his hat in a flourish. "Captain Malmsbury, Number One."

When he stepped down from the curricle, Diana recognized the full regalia of the Four Horse Club with its gaudy striped waistcoat and drab coat down to his ankles. His curricle was yellow-lacquered and new, with brown leather upholstery and brass lanterns.

So, no expense spared.

She'd heard so many stories of Malmsbury's risky behavior that she almost felt she knew him. Pip told stories of the time he had forced a carriage full of people off the road when he tried to overtake a wagon on a corner. Or worse, when her father had refused to sell him one of their horses in front of everyone at Tattersalls.

His reputation was the stuff of infamy rather than legend. It predisposed her to dislike him even before he threw his haughty stare around the courtyard to see who had witnessed his arrival.

"Oh, isn't he handsome." Beth said breathlessly.

Diana rolled her eyes. "We'll see. I never trust anyone in the Four Horse Club. They seem far too impressed with themselves."

As if to prove her point, the captain began barking orders to the ostlers, shouting at them to hurry and that there was a shilling in it for them if they did. He then called over to Diana's groom, who was standing against the wall, and instructed him to fetch some ale.

She bristled.

"Diana, don't," Beth whispered.

But she couldn't help herself. She rushed outside, Beth following on her heels. "I'm afraid he is under my employ, not yours. If he brings anyone ale, it will be me."

He turned to look at her, his glare turning into a wide, delighted and smarmy smile, recognition lighting his eyes. It was not unusual for racing men to recognize her. All the Beau Monde knew Equinox only ran for her. That made her lucky in many a man's eye. "Miss Kingsley, as I live and breathe. I hear you bring good luck." He took in the entirety of her being in one slow look.

Strange man. "My luck is not for you, sir."

"Captain," he corrected her, then shrugged. "I shall do well enough without it." He turned his attention back to his equipment. The groom was having trouble with the horse he was hooking up to the curricle, who reared in all directions and refused the bit.

"How well matched are these two?" the captain asked, his voice curt.

"I've given you the best two we have, as you requested."

"I suppose that is not saying a great deal," Beth said under her voice.

"I hope they steer him into a ditch," Diana said. "Although that's not very sporting of me, I can't help but think he has a wonderful start leaving so early. But there may be hope—for we have the most beautifully matched pairs all the way to Brighton."

Driving a curricle, the matching of your horses was imperative because the vehicle relied on a pole between the horses that was attached to a bar across the saddles. The closer the horses were in height and stride, the faster and smoother the drive.

"And a whip who knows how to drive them to an inch," Beth added, with a small happy sigh.

Diana detected a note of pride in Beth's voice. She turned to look at her friend, and the warmth in Beth's eyes betrayed her. "Yes, Pip is an excellent whip."

She saw the captain have a quick word with the ostler, then he leaped into his carriage and left with a great "rar".

Diana rolled her eyes. "Anyone that has to be so demonstrative with his team does not know horses as well as he says he does. Father launches his team with naught more than a kiss in the air."

Beth put an arm around Diana's shoulder, knowing well that the comment was borne of her frustration at not being able to ride herself. They went back into the inn and had barely poured their tea when the next arrival made a rumpus. Diana looked at the clock on the mantle above the bar.

"If it took Captain Full-of-Himself just under two hours to make it from London. We should look for Templeton in an hour or so." They drank their tea, Beth retrieved her book from their room, and Diana amused herself by playing solitaire with a deck of cards Beth had brought down for her. She did, however, keep a close eye on the courtyard and each of the entrants as they arrived. Two, three, four and five, each of them spaced between fifteen to twenty minutes apart, meaning that everyone was keeping good time.

"I am glad Pip is only half an hour after Templeton," Beth said. "I don't think I could stand waiting here all day for them like this!"

"Yes, we shall be on our way to Brighton as soon as Pip is gone and our carriage is ready. We shall have our own much quieter and slower race. I will have to give instructions to the grooms at each stage to take the horses back to London, but after that, we are free to go." Diana abandoned her game and pulled the cards into a stack. "Come, let us wait in the courtyard. He won't be far away."

Templeton arrived in just over an hour, his team gliding into the courtyard in total harmony. *Beautifully done.* He drove to an inch and her heart burst with pride.

But the action by the staff at the inn could not have been

more different. Instead of ostlers jumping to attention as they had with the captain, the men were nowhere to be seen. Templeton looked around, eager to make the change, but seeing nobody who could help him.

"What manner of mischief is this?" Diana said.

"They're not helping him!" Beth said, outraged.

Before she'd even completed the thought, Diana rushed to the stables. "Daniel! Jeremy!"

Her two grooms stood to attention from the crates they were sitting on. "Yes, ma'am? He's not here, is he?"

"No, Lord Templeton is, and he needs help." She strode past them as they ran to the courtyard. She found two of the ostlers grooming the captain's horses. "Gentleman, what say you bring the Earl of Templeton his horses?"

One man raised his eyebrows in surprise. "Is he here then, is he? Time must have gotten away from us."

"Indeed. Best you catch up with it." She waited, glaring, until they got Templeton's horses.

"Those two? I think not," Diana said. "He will have the pair in the last stall if you please."

"But, ma'am, they're spoken for."

"Yes, for Lord Templeton. Or shall I tell Gentleman Jackson about your lack of sportsmanship today? Would he be impressed? I believe he is coming to buy some horses from my father, Beau Kingsley, next month."

He wasn't, of course, but that didn't mean he never had. Now the ostlers took her seriously, though, which made her mad that she'd had to use her father's name for them to do so.

They ran into the courtyard, where Templeton had jumped down from his curricle and was at his horses' heads while her grooms unhitched them.

The new horses were put in place with a swiftness that was only outdone by the obsequiousness of the ostlers, who knew the name Kingsley as any horse-mad man did.

Templeton had little time but came to her side before he launched himself back up into the curricle. "Thank you, Di," he said, forgetting that they were not currently on such familiar terms. But the childhood nickname sounded so familiar and sweet that she had to nod and wave him away so he didn't see the bloom on her cheeks.

These ridiculous sporting events always made her far too emotional. Her heart knew better than to be moved by Templeton or read too much into his familiarities. But oh, how she wanted to.

She pulled her mind back to the task at hand. Waiting for Pip. "Beth, stop wringing your hands and help me make sure everything is ready."

They both looked up as another entrant, who announced himself to be number seven, Mr. William Cromwell, came and left the courtyard in a flurry of activity.

Diana couldn't stop her eyes darting up the road while Beth paced back and forth. Then, to add to the confusion and the anxiety, Pip did not arrive next as he was supposed to, but it was contestant number nine, Mr. Oliver, who should definitely have been *after* Pip and not before him.

Diana rushed to the man, who was also having trouble getting the ostler's attention. "Did you pass Pip Kingsley on the road?"

His head whipped around. "Yes, I passed him a few miles back on the hill." He frowned. "I'm not sure he was quite the thing."

"Why?" Diana asked.

Beth took her hand and squeezed it. "I'm sure he's fine. He'll be here soon."

Diana shook her head. "No, we'll send someone out to meet him." She caught her groom's gaze. "Daniel, can you find him? You might need to lead the team, if Pip is hurt."

He nodded and raced off toward the stables to find a mount.

Diana and Beth stood at the tollgate on the corner of High Street and Carshalton Road, looking as far as the horizon would allow them. Before Daniel could leave, a vehicle came into view. As it drew slowly closer, Diana spotted the distinctive yellow of Pip's curricle.

"Here he is," Diana said and exhaled. He was upright. He was well. She peered closer, and her heart lurched. Was he?

"Something's wrong," Beth added. She wrung her hands.

Pip traveled slowly. "Perhaps there was something wrong with his tackle, or the shaft." If that were the case, he could take her curricle. It may not be so fast, but at least it was whole.

Daniel arrived by her side, lifting a hand to act as a visor against the sun. "Why, it looks like James is driving," he exclaimed in confusion.

Diana squinted. "I believe you're right. I wonder what on earth has happened?" The curricle limped into the courtyard, and the reason for its awkwardness was soon apparent. James, the groom, was handling the ribbons while supporting Pip. The latter was a dead weight against the groom's side, his head lolling around and smearing blood over Jimmy's livery.

Beth drew in a shocked breath and took a few steps backward with her hand over her heart.

Oh, no. She turned to an ostler. "Please, good sir, have someone fetch a physician." He nodded, his concerned gaze taking in Pip's lifeless form. There was no time for hysterics. Diana strode forward while the grooms pulled Pip from the curricle.

The groom jumped down, wild-eyed and with a gash on his cheek that had rivulets of blood running down his face. "We were driving up the hill, through an avenue of trees, when out of nowhere, a massive branch fell into the curricle. It got Pip square on the noggin. He was out cold immediately, and there's me trying to get myself into the front seat to help him with the ribbons. He's been coming to and dropping out again ever since. I'm fine, though. It mostly missed me."

There was little wind today, but it may have been different a few miles down the road. Diana still couldn't keep the skepticism out of her voice. "So, a branch fell from the tree at the very time you drove under it." There was no point alarming the groom, though, especially if Pip were to wake up and want to continue the race. "Well, I suppose these things happen."

Beth frowned. "It seems awfully unlucky."

Pip had gashes on his face made by the falling branch. "I should like to have seen that branch," Diana said to Beth in a hush. She imagined the end of it neatly sawn.

"I am going to make sure the doctor is coming," Beth said. "I'll be back soon."

Pip, who was being held up under the shoulders by the two grooms, chose that moment to come to. He opened his eyes sleepily. "Threw it out," he said. "Damn thing almost killed me."

"And where is your hat? Smashed to pieces?" Diana asked. "Or were you driving without it again?" She pulled his valise from the back of the curricle. He would need it.

"Without," he said with a sleepy smile. "Can't admonish me … too sick."

She inspected his head with tenderness. There was one lump, maybe two, already formed and a shallow gash that still bled. "Ugh, you are an annoying specimen."

"And I have lost Equinox for us," he said sadly.

Diana frowned. "Goodness, don't think on that for a moment," she replied. "We'll get him back, I promise you." She grabbed his hand and squeezed it. "Now, no more talking. We will wait for the physician."

"I keep telling you … perfectly fine," Pip said. "Fully conscious. Able to go on." He groaned. "I must continue … The prince …"

Her stomach squirmed with nerves. The prince owned Equinox. "The prince what? Out with it."

Pip's lips pinched together. "He's going to sell our boy as soon as the hay settles on the stables. To some sheik."

She drew in a shocked breath, and then that breath disappeared and she couldn't seem to breathe at all. She dropped his hand. "What? How could he do that?"

He nodded and then slumped. "I *must* win."

"Or *I* must," she replied darkly, looking down the road. She had to hurry, the next entrant would be arriving soon.

Pip tried to stand on his own, but gave up and leaned on the grooms. "You're scaring me."

"Am I? Too bad, I'm racing." The words tumbled out before she had even thought them, like they had a life of their own. Run the race to Brighton? The very thing she had told herself she was, under no circumstances, to do. But these were exceptional circumstances, surely?

"But your reputation has only just recovered from Fortescue. Think of Colonel Webster," he said weakly.

Diana took a deep, excited breath. Pip had started the race as the Beau Kingsley entrant. She could finish it.

I shouldn't.

I definitely shouldn't.

"But you're not listening to me," Pip said.

The grooms snickered.

"I am going to drive this race, and I am going to win." She turned to Daniel, who was still supporting Pip. "Could you please put Pip down inside and come straight back out to change the horses?"

Daniel nodded. "Yes, Miss Kingsley."

She followed them inside, where she threw everything into her valise. Pip shook off his greatcoat and lay on the bed. "If you must be a fool, at least put my clothes on so you don't draw the attention of every man from here to the pavilion." He groaned and sank into the pillows.

She put his valise on the floor and pulled out a fresh shirt and breeches. "Surely wearing your clothes will only garner *more* attention," she said dryly.

"Lock that hair away, put my hat on, and with your height you could carry anything off. Especially if you wear my greatcoat." He tried to sit up, yelped, and lay back down again.

It wasn't the worst idea he'd ever had. But at least there was half a chance that if she was in disguise, she might actually avoid all detection.

His eyes were closed, but he waved his hand around vaguely. "They'll be looking for me, remember, not you. Just acquit yourself as I would and hope to Hades you don't meet anyone I know."

She was woefully unprepared. But if she didn't win, Equinox would be gone forever. It was up to her now.

She ignored the bubbling joy and pure glee that burst inside her heart.

It most certainly was not to be trusted.

CHAPTER 12

FROM SUTTON TO REIGATE. ELEVEN MILES OF DRIVING PERFECTION—IF SHE DID SAY SO HERSELF

Diana, dressed in Pip's clothing, crossed the dusty courtyard with long strides and her head down to avoid the ostlers. She handed her valise to Daniel so he could strap it in. The groom took in her ensemble with a small smile, his eyes bright with excitement. "Let's win this, Mr. Kingsley."

She had expected grudging service from him, not this full-blown support. "Thank you, Daniel," she said, her voice gruff from the lump that was forming in her throat. It gave her a new determination to win; for Equinox, Pip, and everyone who worked at their estate. She went to the horses. They were straining against their bits and definitely ready to go.

She briskly checked the tackle and when everything was in order, put one glossy black boot onto the step, admiring its shine. They were a touch big, but the feel of the leather all the way up her calf was incredibly comforting. The breeches, on the other hand, were the opposite. How on earth did men survive with their bottoms ensconced so tightly?

Beth had followed her out, arms crossed and a look none too

"

happy on her face. "Ready to ride, *Mr.* Kingsley?" She said it with a definite edge. "You are gambling with your future here."

Diana pulled herself into the curricle. "I'll gamble everything to get him back." She sat and took the ribbons, threading them gently through her fingers. This may be a race, but she had no intention of treating these horses any differently than she normally would. If she were to win or catch up the time that Pip had lost, through no fault of his own, then it would be done through driving smartly, not at her horses' expense. They were far too precious to her for that.

"Please. If you see Templeton might win, let him win and leave the race. He would buy Equinox with the winnings and at least then you know he is safe." Her eyes were pleading.

"Pooh," Diana replied. "As if Templeton would be so considerate. He'd just blow the winnings on waistcoats and new boots."

"You do him an injustice, I think," Beth said.

And on those damning words, Diana set the horses to with a gentle kissing sound that they knew so well from her.

Let Templeton win, indeed. She would never live it down.

The road from Sutton climbed steadily uphill, so Diana took her team out easy. There would be plenty of time for them to run out their jitters later. Just in front there was a wagon filled with hessian sacks and four men riding on top of them. She overtook them smartly, before there was oncoming traffic to contend with.

The sun hid behind a bank of clouds, which was something to be happy about. There was nothing worse than trying to drive to an inch with the sun in your eyes.

Daniel sat on the small seat in the rear, his driving bugle, or "yard of tin" as Pip would call it, at the ready. Excitement rode the air, from the horses' flicking ears and their steady but barely contained trot, to the wide smile she couldn't quite keep from her face. Did she look like a gentleman racer? Would she pass muster when examined?

They soon found their rhythm as they left the village and met with the open fields and pastures leading them to the top of Reigate Hill. Diana kept her team to a simple brisk trot, careful not to let them overextend on the downhill run.

It was hard not to let them go, though, as the wind rushed past her face and the sheer exhilaration of driving a curricle with two beautiful horses picked her up and carried her away. The truth was that Sally and Lofty would run and run and run until their dear legs gave out beneath them, because they were a wonderful pair of horses. So it was entirely up to Diana to make sure she protected them.

In the distance, she spotted a large carriage, most likely a stage or a mail coach. It had luggage strapped to the top and people spilling out of the windows and sitting on the roof. If she peered closely, there was a sporting curricle sitting directly behind it, obviously trying to pass.

It looked like Mr. Oliver, entrant nine who had overtaken Pip. Could she dare to hope she had caught up with him already?

From her vantage point, she saw a steady stream of oncoming traffic that would stop the curricle from overtaking the stagecoach. This was her chance to make up some of the time they had lost at the inn. Holding the reins carefully, she pulled the spyglass from its strap and handed it back to her groom. "Daniel, look ahead and tell me when the next break in the traffic is so that I can overtake."

"Overtake what?" Daniel stared ahead. "Ah, I see. The curricle and the stagecoach." He paused. "Brave."

She would never risk her horses, and she would never let them take flight at a point on the road where it was neither safe nor prudent. However, she was never going to win this race by taking the most careful and safe route. It was all a matter of judging the risks.

She looked ahead, assessing which point in the distance would be the safest to attempt the coup. Oncoming was a large wagon loaded with hay bales. Once it passed them, there would be a big enough gap. Just. "After the wagon with the hay bales. What think you?"

"I agree," Daniel said. "Otherwise we'll be stuck behind the stagecoach too."

The horses were keen to increase their speed and their frustration travelled up the reins in fits and bursts. But she kept a steadfast pace, gaining on the stagecoach and curricle.

The oncoming wagon was getting closer, so she started to increase her speed. She was close enough to see that a man with a red kerchief around his neck drove the wagon, when Mr. Oliver heard her coming. He turned, his eyes wide under his crown beaver hat as he took in the speed at which she was approaching.

Yes, he should definitely be scared, for she was about to overtake him.

Then, with no regard to his own safety, or that of his horses, he pulled out from behind the coach and started to overtake, putting himself directly in the path of the hay wagon. She drew in a shocked breath at his sheer folly.

The hay wagon was heavy and had four horses pulling it. There was no way it could stop in time, or likely even slow.

"Mr. Oliver, no!" Diana watched in horror as the racer committed to overtaking the stagecoach instead of pulling his head back in, as any sane person would have.

The men on top of the coach shouted, a woman inside screamed, and the coachman probably didn't say anything at all because he was too busy trying to slow his team to give the fool as much chance of passing as possible.

Miraculously, the stagecoach slowed, and the curricle slipped in front of it by the absolute barest of margins.

Diana breathed a sigh of relief, while behind her Daniel uttered a soft oath. But perhaps they were both too quick to exhale because the curricle swayed alarmingly and looked for all the world as if it were about to topple over. The horses veered to the left and ran off the road.

Diana caught up to both vehicles at a smart pace. Loud cheers came from the stagecoach as it passed the curricle.

Then a minute later Diana passed him too. The large red wheel was little more than spokes and splintered wood, but the horses were standing, and he was at least working to unhitch them.

"We should stop," Diana said, eying him warily. He looked very angry, his fists raised to the air, cursing nobody in particular except perhaps the fate and stupidity that had led him into the mud.

"I would rather we didn't," Daniel replied. "His horses are fine, and he looks testy."

Diana slowed Sally and Lofty, mulling it over. But her mind was completely made up when they did pass and he hurled a string of abuse at them.

"We'll leave him to his own devices," Diana said. "What a creative vocabulary."

Diana took a much more circumspect attack at passing the coach. She waited until she reached a long flat piece of road with fields of very uninterested sheep on either side—without oncoming vehicles.

As she passed, the coachman raised his whip to her in salute. She raised hers in return and carried on through the parkland, on the downhill descent. This area was familiar. It meant they were close to Merstham and their next change. She increased her speed, passing more vehicles while the going was good. The horses were well worn in now, and itching to be sprung. She obliged them for a little while, knowing they could have a good rest in Merstham.

How soon would it be until she caught up with Alec?

She couldn't wait to see his face as she passed him.

The morning cloud had burned off, leaving a sunny morning. There was very little in the way of wind. A thrill of excitement ran through her as they progressed surely and steadily toward

Reigate, keeping tight control over her pair. The Surrey fields were a patchwork of green and late-summer gold, bordered by trees, and the hills a hazy blue on the horizon. She took a deep breath as an unnamed happiness welled in her chest. Love for the freedom of the road? Her horses? Who knew? All she did know was that in that moment, Equinox was going to be fine, and the man she was going to marry would certainly come to love her.

"Is that Lord Templeton on the hill?" Daniel said. "I suspect he might put a stop to us racing." His voice had an edge of *and I should like to see him try*, that Diana could not help but admire.

She slowed the team and lifted her spyglass. Few people had a robin's egg blue curricle, which had been a twenty-first birthday present from his father. He had called upon them that birthday, his face bursting with excitement, and taken both she and Pip for a drive around Hyde Park. She remembered looking at the murky water of the Serpentine and wondering if, now that he was of age, he might offer for her.

He had not.

"That is definitely Templeton." Of course, being the busy road to Brighton, there were now many vehicles between her and the bright-blue curricle. The question was whether to catch Alec or whether to keep him safely in front of her. None the wiser. "I don't think we will catch him. He'll spring his horses as soon as he crests the hill." Even now, the distance between them was barely closing. He could likely see another racer ahead of him and was doing his best to overtake.

By some miracle, they came upon him less than half a mile before the turnpike at Lower Kingswood. He was still driving at an astonishing pace, and any attempt to pass him would be risky. But she had to do it before the gate.

"I'm going to spring the horses. Hold on!" Diana shouted, then urged the horses faster and then faster again until they drew alongside Alec's curricle.

There was no point trying to hide who she was because he

would know the moment he looked up that Pip was not driving the curricle. So, with a great deal of satisfaction, she tipped Pip's hat and smiled as she blasted past him, keeping her horses perfectly under control the entire time. She had the satisfaction of watching his eyes widen in disbelief and then the rapid blinking of his confusion. Whether the confusion related to her driving Pip's curricle, or that she had passed him so easily, it was hard to tell. But he should expect no less of her.

He would be impressed. She knew it.

As they approached the gate, Daniel let out an exuberant bugle blast, and the tollgate slowly swung open.

She had told him she had a few secrets up her sleeve for Pip, and it was hardly her fault if he had not thought of them. Besting him only increased the jubilant mood that lasted her the next four miles to The Old Angel in Woodhatch, a few miles short of the halfway mark.

The old Tudor inn stood on the edge of the township, surrounded by trees and a charming rustic vista. A mother goose led her goslings into a nearby pond, honking and flapping. Two children played with a branch and a ball, and the air carried the smell of freshly baked bread. It was all much more relaxed than her racing heart would allow.

The courtyard was curiously quiet. No ostler came out to greet her, and her grooms were nowhere to be seen. She climbed down from the box, and Daniel took the horses' heads while she went to investigate.

She found her grooms asleep on a mound of hay. Elsewhere, grooms and ostlers were busy at work. She stopped one, only remembering at the last moment to make her voice as low as possible.

She was a man, after all. A man would expect answers. *Now.* "Can you please explain why my men are asleep?"

"Don't know 'em, sir." He shook her off and kept walking.

She leaned over one groom, shaking his shoulder. "Thomas!"

He snored in reply, and a glass of elderberry wine she hadn't noticed on his lap tipped over. She watched in dismay as the dark liquid poured over him.

Did it have a sleeping draft in it? It was so unlike a Kingsley man to drink while on the job, but if someone was offered free wine, what kind of man could resist? Yet a little wine was not enough to have them pass out. No. The wine must have been tampered with.

Now what was she to do? A simple sleeping draft would just wear off over time, and there was nothing she could do to hasten the effect. She strode to an older man, whom she'd seen giving orders.

"Sir. My men are inebriated. I will ensure my father, Beau Kingsley, is informed if either are mistreated in any way."

A bear-like paw clapped her on the back, pushing her forward a foot. "Lad, I watched them drink the wine myself. Now they're having a kip. I'll make sure they come to rights, although I'm sure there'll be hell to pay when your father finds out you had to change your horses yourself."

"Hell to pay indeed," Diana replied. She went to the stall, where she found the horses, completely unprepared for the road. "Damnation," she cursed under her breath, and put their tackle in place for the ride.

She worked as quickly as she could, but when she led the horses back into the forecourt, it was to find Alec's team pulling up. She may have lost the time she made up, but just seeing his familiar form, someone she could trust completely when it was obvious crooks surrounded her, had her heart skipping a merry beat.

At least she hoped it was relief, and not admiration at the way he drove his team like a nonpareil and glided to a halt beside her.

He jumped down from the box in the way only a six-foot man could do with great grace. He was so focused on what he had to say that he didn't notice her distress, or the fact she was changing the horses herself. "You charged through that gate like Hades!"

"Yes, I did. But, Templeton, my grooms have been drugged."

He stopped short, his eyes narrowed as he took in the entire forecourt scene. All outrage at her clever race tactics evaporated. "You tried to wake them?"

"Yes. They're out cold," she said. "Daniel and I are doing the change."

"I see. Let's get your horses changed as quickly as possible and get out of here."

Nobody had approached him to change his horses, but he got the attention of the same ostler who had brushed off Diana's earlier complaint. "Sir. Please have my horses brought out and changed."

"I'll get there, sir," he said slowly.

He took a step toward the ostler. "You'll get there *now*."

Diana shuddered at the command in his voice. But it was more than that. His entire being vibrated with the power he normally kept tightly coiled. The ostler took a step back, frowning. They both felt that his power could be unleashed at any moment. *Who knew Templeton could be so masterful?* She blinked. This time her heart was *definitely* beating faster for Templeton alone.

The ostler mumbled but turned on his heel and went to the stables quicker than Diana had seen him move since she arrived. She'd be envious of how quickly he'd gotten action if she wasn't so impressed.

He turned to her, concern in his eyes and all hint of annoyance gone. "Come, let's hitch these two up while you tell me what happened to Pip. I know you didn't want to ride this race, and yet here you are."

Just the way he looked at her, with frankness and a levelness that told her he trusted her instincts and her decisions, made her want to throw her arms around him. Which was not perhaps the correct etiquette for a young gentleman with another young gentleman. So instead, she took a deep breath and checked the girth buckles on both horses. "I'll tell you directly after I recover from your newly discovered heroic side."

He looked up from where he was settling the pole between the horses and tilted his head to one side, blinking slowly in that lazy way he had when he was ready to be amused.

She pretended to pull some smelling salts from the pocket of Pip's greatcoat and inhale a little. Then she affected a shudder and turned back to him with a bright smile. "Phew. Very well. I am recovered."

CHAPTER 13

IN WHICH ALEC REALISES HE HAS TOO MUCH TO LOSE TO BE IN THIS FOOL'S RACE

Alec turned to Diana, unsure what he'd done to appear heroic in her eyes. How was he to repeat it if he had no notion?

The strange thing was, being just as tall as Pip and dressed in his many caped greatcoat, she looked both practical and increasingly feminine at the same time. He liked it. But then, she'd look good in anything. She moved as though she'd been set free to do exactly as she pleased. Loose and athletic.

It was too bad that was a terrible idea.

Her groom rolled the curricle toward the horses, and Alec guided it into place. "What happened to Pip?" Because nothing short of an accident would make his friend drop out of the race.

"A branch fell on his head," she replied quietly, threading the strap through the eye of the rod and buckling it. "He has a big lump on his head and is still at The Cock. Beth is looking after him, and I expect them to continue on to Brighton as soon as the doctor has cleared him. Alec, I—"

Alec went to the horses' heads and put their bridles on, carefully placing the bits in their mouths. "I still do not see the reason you had to continue the race for him. I know I encouraged you to begin with, but you convinced me it would be a disastrous course of action. Unless you truly do not want to marry Colonel Webster."

He couldn't keep the hint of hope from his voice, but her eyes widened in alarm. "Colonel Webster may think it a great lark and still want to marry me. Not all men are high sticklers."

The hand she let fall back to her side was trembling. *Diana Kingsley, trembling.*

Alec looked at her in alarm. He could think of nothing that would cause the level of anxiety that thrummed from her. She was always so brave. It made him want to pull her into his arms. But that was not his place.

He tried again as he threaded the reins through the bit. Daniel was doing the same to the other horse. "Please rethink this. You haven't been discovered. You can go back to The Cock and be with Pip, nobody any the wiser." He couldn't bear it if she were hurt, either socially or physically, by this race. And there were definitely some below-board goings on this day.

As though divining his thoughts, she grabbed his hand.

He looked down at it as though her hand in his were the most confusing thing he had ever seen. Indeed, it caused him to lose both his breath and all coherent thought for a good few moments. "There is nothing you can say and nothing you can do that will stop me."

The ostler brought out his horses. They had their harnesses on and were ready to be put to, thank heaven. "Move faster please, lads," he said sharply, and his own groom took charge of them, getting the curricle hitched up to the fresh horses.

If somebody was prepared to tamper with the elderberry wine, then who knew what else they were capable of doing. He turned to Diana. "We should keep close for the next stage at the very least. There's no point going as fast as we can if neither of us actually make it to Brighton."

"I couldn't agree more," Diana said. He was relieved to see that rather than being stubborn about it, she seemed to be just as worried as he was.

She had called him Alec, not Templeton, and had taken his hand. She really *was* distressed.

"Then, if one of us sees something untoward, we use the yard of tin and blow on it as hard as we can to alert the other, perhaps we can both get through this safely."

She smiled, obviously relieved he was taking her seriously. "I didn't know you cared."

He raised what he hoped was an insouciant eyebrow. "I do not care. You are a grave annoyance and a danger to everyone around you. And for the love of God, don't outstrip me and be in front. If a branch is going to fall from a tree, let it fall on me. There is plenty of time for you to catch up on the last stage. Let's hide your light behind a bushel for a short while."

She looked at him teasingly. "You truly *do* care."

He ignored her. "And while we're at it," he said, beckoning her closer, "your masculine appearance needs some help. Come here." He reached forward and fluffed her cravat until it covered the place where her Adam's apple would have been if she were a man. But her neck was delicate and her skin against his hands was soft in a way no man's would ever be. He blinked slowly feeling like he'd had a gulp of that elderberry wine himself. And then, seeing the blush rise up her cheeks, he stepped back and admired his handiwork, as though touching her had not affected him. "You must tuck that hair in a little better."

"Very well," she replied, her voice grave.

Daniel had finished hooking the horses up. Alec automatically offered his hand to help her up, then realized that was something he would do for Miss Diana Kingsley, but not her brother. He let the hand fall to his side.

He must make one last attempt. "Can I convince you to give this race up now? Nothing is as it should be."

She raised her chin and shook her head. "Thank you, no." She lifted her hand in salute. "See you in Brighton for the ball I am not attending." She kissed the air, and the horses responded.

"No! Wait!" He scrambled after the curricle. But with great aplomb and dashing style, she sprang her horses.

"I was supposed to go first," he said to her fast-retreating form.

He shook his head and left the inn smartly. He had to catch up with her and then keep up with her. The nervous pit in his stomach told him this race was about to become less about restoring his fortune and more about ensuring Diana got through it unscathed. He looked up at the sky and sent up a quick prayer that he was wrong.

He let his horses go faster than he normally would in an effort to catch her. It wasn't hard, as she knew how to pace her team to perfection and was going at a steady pace rather than the breakneck pace he'd adopted to get ahead of her. As he passed, she nodded and lifted her whip, as though in acknowledgement of the fact they had agreed he should lead.

He pulled in ahead of her and slowed his team down to a steadier pace.

Eyes narrowed, he scanned the road ahead, looking for trouble. The problem was, the road ahead was a maze of small hills and switchbacks that wound their way through Earlswood Common. It was pretty countryside, undulating into the distance, but it could hide any number of things.

A thought that had his stomach churning.

His tack had been cut.

Pip had been hit by a falling branch.

Her grooms had been drugged.

Someone had planned a series of traps along the road, and he and Diana were likely riding into another. Diana might have paid the tollgate masters along the route, but someone else had been equally industrious.

Alec was caught between worrying about her and admiration

of her bravery. The way her chin had lifted in defiance, whip in hand and a flush on her cheeks. But admiration had to come in second place, for Pip would never forgive him if a hair on his sister's head was harmed.

Worse still, he would never forgive himself.

Discovering the lengths someone was going to to win this race should put an end to it for him, and for her. He had too many people at home relying on him, and she had a fiancé waiting to start married life. They both had too much to lose to get caught up in this fool's game.

And he was quite sure the road wasn't finished with them yet.

Within a few miles of leaving Earlswood Common, Alec could already see he had strayed too far ahead of Diana. Times where he had overtaken vehicles and assumed she would follow suit, only to find the conditions had not been quite right for her, and she was left behind.

A few miles ahead, the road started into a gradual decline that ended in their next change at Horley, which would be the best chance for her to catch up. He wasn't worried. There had been nothing in the last few miles to pique his very alert senses. She was behind him. All appeared to be in order.

He was just wondering whether he should pull over and wait, when a lady came to his attention by the side of the road. Dressed in thin muslin with a straw bonnet, she was holding her ankle and howling. There was no way in the world this was something that Alec could drive by. The bonus would be that stopping would give Diana a chance to catch up to him. She would know what to do with a lady in distress far better than him.

His mind made up, he slowed his horses and maneuvered them to the grassy side of the road, his groom jumping down to go to the horses' heads. If it was in his power to take her up with him in the small space there was on the curricle's seat, he would do so. The lady did not look up, engrossed in her own agony.

"Excuse me, miss," he said. "Can I be of assistance?"

Stephen, his groom, grumbled. "Careful, my lord. Could be shenanigans. Many a lady can fit a pistol in her reticule."

Wise words, but Alec could see tears streaming down her wet face. "I hardly think a woman in a straw bonnet with a twisted ankle is a trap," he said.

She looked up, her luminous eyes shining with tears. "Oh, could you help me, dear sir? I was walking into the village to see the vicar and his family for lunch. I was reading at the same time and then I twisted my ankle. Now I can't walk and am relying on the kindness of a stranger."

Alec scanned the surrounds. She was very handily situated where there was a drive off the road that seemed to lead to a farmhouse. He wondered briefly why she had not limped to the farmhouse. He jumped down from the seat to better help her up into the curricle. "I will take you into the village and drop you at the vicarage," he said.

As he approached she smiled, not a grateful and sweet smile but a knowing one, the kind he imagined a cat would make just before it sank its claws into a mouse. As if to prove the point, she pulled a small pistol from underneath the book she had on her lap. Her tears dried up instantly.

"If you could step farther away from your carriage and toward the tree, sir," she said, her voice a strange mix of upper class and flower-selling urchin from St. Paul's.

"Devil take it," Alec said. "There's no need to shoot me. I have only a few shillings for the tollgate in valuables."

"I'm not interested in your *valuables*," she said. "And I won't shoot you, but I will shoot your horse, if you don't mind."

"Mind?" The question made him so angry he could feel red clouding his eyes. "I will do anything as long as you don't hurt my horses."

"Or your groom," Stephen said.

"And of course my groom," Alec added, rolling his eyes. He was a lummox, a patsy, a Bartholomew's child, a greenling. Taken in by a crying lady.

She smiled, bringing out an enchanting dimple. Damn her eyes. "You gentlemen are always so dependable when it comes to your horses. I vow we women would be better off if we were horses ourselves."

She didn't take her eyes off him, but Alec made sure to look over her shoulder, pretend to see something coming, and then shoot his gaze back to her as if he didn't want her to notice. It didn't work. She just laughed. "I won't look around, if that's what you're thinking. I'm not a newborn."

No, *she* was not gullible. He was the gullible one.

"If you're not robbing me, what *are* you doing? Being paid to slow me down?"

"Perhaps." She laughed. "But don't be tempted into thinking I won't shoot your leg if you run."

"I would, of course, rather you did not. And I'm sure you'd rather not hang for shooting a peer." He was in all kinds of trouble and, worse still, Diana would be caught up in all this, too, in just a few minutes.

"We'll just tie you up, then. Douglas!"

We?

A huge man, who had the nose of a boxer and the build of an outhouse, walked from behind a tree a few feet away and stood behind her. "Is this the one?"

"It's one of the ones. Who cares?" She suddenly lapsed into a Cockney accent that perfectly matched his. "But he's saying he's a lord, so don't bruise him just in case."

Douglas took a menacing step toward him, swinging a cudgel in one hand and a rope in the other.

The sound of a single shot ripped through the peaceful countryside.

What now?

Alec dropped to the ground and craned his neck around to see Diana some distance away, bunched reins in one hand and a smoking pistol in the other.

The lady yelped and dropped her gun. Behind her, Douglas swore and clutched his arm, his rope and cudgel falling to the ground.

Two for one bullet?

She inspected her hand, and finding it unharmed, turned to her accomplice. "Douglas!"

Alec took the opportunity to retrieve her gun. It now sported a dent on the barrel but was fully loaded. *Damnation.* It was not a bluff. She really *could* have shot him.

He strode to where she leaned over her accomplice and twisted her arm around, pulling her away from him. Stephen walked the horses to a nearby tree and secured them. "Shall I tie her up, my lord?"

Alec motioned to the rope on the ground. "Yes. With that. I'll get more rope from the carriage, and we can tie Douglas up, too. Then we'll check his wound. He may need the surgeon. Also, I shot him, not Mr. Kingsley, got it?"

Stephen nodded and tied the woman's hands together behind her back, leading her away. "Can we get *her* to agree to that?"

She was crying uncontrollably in earnest now, while Douglas was telling her none too gently to "shut her cake hole" as he sank himself against the trunk of a tree. "She doesn't know what happened at the moment."

But he did. Good Lord, Diana had just shot a man for him. It was pandemonium. But when Alec blinked, his world slowed as Diana rode toward them like heaven's fury. Her horses were perfectly in control, her hat off and her golden hair blowing in the wind like she was some kind of avenging angel.

His heart skipped more beats than was comfortable and landed with a thud in the soles of his shoes.

What man could live without a woman like that? Beau

Kingsley be damned and her fiancé be damned. He could no longer pretend he didn't want her.

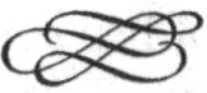

CHAPTER 14

IN WHICH BEGGING FORGIVENESS IS SUPERIOR TO ASKING PERMISSION

Diana arrived in time to see Alec pick up the pistol the lady had dropped to the ground and put it in his curricle.

She slowed her horses to a stop, her heart thumping for all it was worth. The birds still chirped in the trees, and the clouds rolled across the sky like nothing happened.

But she'd shot a man.

He wasn't dead. He moved his head, propped up against a large oak. But even the simplest gunshot wound could kill, and this man's life was now in her hands. It felt like it was.

She shuddered.

Father was right in everything he ever said about her. There had been no thinking, no decision-making, before she'd raised that gun. All she saw was Alec, with a gun trained on him and a large man stalking him, cudgel in hand.

In the space of seconds, she yelled "pistol!" to Daniel, bunched her reins in one hand, and shot with the other.

No thought involved.

She was rash, heedless, thoughtless, and now there would be

magistrates, hearings, and perhaps imprisonment. This went beyond the ruin of her good reputation.

This was the ruin of *her life.*

What, then, was this detachment? Where was the panic? Instead, it was like the whole thing was happening to someone else, and her mind was watching like an impartial bystander.

Alec walked to the side of her curricle and held up a hand to help her down. She took it. His grip was warm and strong, and he held on for just a moment longer than he should have.

The warmth of his hand spread up her arm and bloomed in her chest. *All will be well.* She took a deep breath. "I haven't *killed* him, have I?"

Alec clapped her on the shoulder, as though he were greeting a man, his eyes brimming with gratitude. "*You* have done nothing, my dear fellow. Didn't even shoot. *I* had a pistol to defend myself, and it went off." He looked at her with a knowing expression, and she nodded. "In fact, you should just get back in your curricle and drive away. I'll deal with this."

He was going to take the blame for the shot, for everything. Her heart lurched. He was too good. Tears gathered in her eyes. "I can't let you do that."

His eyes gleamed. "You saved my life, therefore this is the very least I can do. Let's just swap pistols."

She gave him her pistol and shot, and he fetched his from his curricle and gave it to her. "Thank you, Alec. I owe you."

He shook his head decisively. "No, I owe *you*. No man of my acquaintance could have shot like that. It was magnificent. How were you so accurate while driving?"

Would this be a good time to shatter his illusions and tell him she was actually aiming at the gun the woman was holding and not the man at all? "Just instinct," she said, curt, hoping he would get the hint to stop talking.

He shook his head in obvious admiration. "Her gun was

loaded and cocked. You shot it out of her hand, then the ricochet got her accomplice Douglas."

"That makes me feel somewhat better." She would love to say she had meant to hit them both. "But this is most vexing. It was obviously a trap."

Diana took a step toward the tree, where Stephen had finished tying up the couple. Douglas sat in a dappled light that did nothing to hide the blood seeping through the cravat Stephen had wrapped around his arm. "Oh, dear."

Alec's groom shrugged, seemingly unconcerned. "He's bleeding a lot, but it's more of a graze, Mr. Kingsley. If we put some salve on it, he'll be right as a trivet and able to see the magistrate."

She walked over to the man. "Then why is he so quiet?"

"Don't get too close, sir," he said. It still sounded strange to have someone call her "sir."

Douglas opened his eyes. "Nobody likes spilling claret when it's their own." Then he swore at her, a stream of curses a sailor would be proud of.

She jumped back, cheeks flaming.

"Lily-livered gentry-mort," Douglas said in disgust, then looked at her more closely. "And you're a lady! Shot by a *lady*!" He swore again and shook his head in obvious disgust.

Alec took long strides toward them. "Ah, Douglas, you've a foul mouth. I shot you, fool." He pulled off his cravat and tied it from the man's mouth around to the back of his head, knotting it tightly. Then he took his flask of brandy and doused the wound, making Douglas groan. "I was going to leave you my flask of brandy to drink, but consider *that* offer rescinded." He smiled at Diana. "No man can swear with that level of fluency if he's on death's door. He's going to be fine."

Easy words, but not necessarily true. Breeze hit her cheek, reminding her she *was* living this. She inhaled deeply, annoyed when the breath was shuddery.

Alec looked at her steadily. "Talk to me."

He did not seem nearly as shaken by the whole incident as she. Instead, he had an air of energy about him. But perhaps having your life threatened by criminals invigorated a man.

She tried, but nothing came out. "I …"

He took her hand as though trying to press his courage into it. "There now. A lively bit of action, but nothing will come of it. Revel in how brave and daring you are. For you are both of those things. I won't let anyone harm you. Trust me."

His gaze drifted from her mouth, to her eyes, and back to her mouth. If anyone else looked at her like that, she would expect an imminent earth-shattering kiss.

Daniel returned, his heavy steps crunching through the undergrowth. "Sir, there are four men tied behind yonder tree. They were racers too." He frowned. "No sign of their horses or vehicles."

Goodness, more victims of the race. Her teeth chattered and she rubbed her hands up and down her arms to warm herself. "I am going to find my hat." It was bad enough that Douglas knew she was a lady.

Alec pointed north. "I see it on the hedge." He turned to Daniel. "Show me." Alec followed Daniel back into the wooded area, while she raced toward Pip's hat, picking it up and dusting it off. She put it on, hiding her hair, and went back, pulling the hat down as far as she could.

Alec and Daniel returned a few moments later with two gentlemen and their grooms, each of them rubbing their wrists, but otherwise unharmed. He raised an eyebrow. "Looks as though I'm not the only widgeon who fell for it."

"Idiocy in numbers, then." They looked like the racers she'd spied from the window at the inn, but it was hard to be sure.

Alec addressed the group. "Introduce yourself, gentlemen, and your race number."

They each bowed in turn.

"Williams, number three."

"Cox, racer four."

"Wiley, number two."

"McKenzie, number five."

The last man bowed. "And me, James Croak, racer number six at your service."

She would never remember all their names, but what did it matter? That was everyone but number eight, the man she had seen run off the road trying to overtake the stagecoach. Each entrants' chances thoroughly ruined, except for Malmsbury. Although perhaps something had also happened to him that they weren't aware of.

Diana leaned in to Alec, turning her back to the group. "We must be off," she said under her breath, not wanting to draw attention to herself. Any of these gentlemen looking too closely at her could be disastrous.

Thankfully, he took the hint. "Could you gentlemen take care of these criminals while we continue with the race?"

Williams, a tall and very thin gentleman with thick, brown eyebrows stepped forward. "At your service, my lord. I'll get my horses and curricle from the farmhouse yonder and fetch the magistrate and the surgeon to have them dealt with. You continue your race. If we don't have a gun aimed at us, I'm sure we can handle this pair."

"Here, here," said the other racers, sounding entirely jubilant about it.

Alec fished into his pocket and pulled out a golden card case. He handed a card to Williams. "Give this to the magistrate and let him know I'll be back this way later tomorrow to give him my statement."

Diana could hardly be outraged with his light-handed treatment of the law when she was the beneficiary of it.

He turned to Diana. "Well, Mr. Kingsley, if I might have a word?"

"Very well," she said, trying to make her voice gruff. She walked toward her curricle and jumped into the seat. Daniel was at the horses' heads, calming them in soothing tones. Templeton stood next to the wheel.

"My dear girl," he said, his eyes pleading. "This race is not worth your safety or mine. I do not believe these dirty tricks aim to permanently injure us; however, they could inadvertently do just that. I am worried."

And there it was. He was going to pull them *both* out of the race. She found small relief that he would give up the race at the same time. "I know you are right, but Templeton, I cannot … I cannot give up." She concentrated on the horses' swishing tails for a few moments. "Pip told me the prince is going to sell Equinox to live overseas. I couldn't bear it."

There was silence for the longest stretch of time.

He took a deep breath and exhaled slowly, muttering under his breath something that sounded like "*If only you would love me the same way you love that big brute.*"

Her heart lurched. He wanted her to love him? She blinked in confusion, not knowing where to look or what to think. "I beg your pardon?"

"I said 'if only your father would buy back the big brute,'" he eventually replied, staring at the wheel and not at her.

"Right." She shook her head, ignoring the nerves fluttering in her stomach. As if Templeton would declare himself! "Firstly, Father has already spent the money on new mares and, secondly, relations between us are strained. Indeed, I am sure they are just as excited to marry me off as I am to be gone. At this point I would have taken an offer from a farmer with three sheep and a goat just to leave."

He reared his head back and exhaled loudly, as though a puzzle had fallen into place. "*Now* your engagement to Colonel Webster makes sense."

She tamped down her irritation at his correct assumption.

"He's a good man, and will take care of me. And I him. I *chose* to marry him of my own free will."

Alec shrugged, his expression suggesting he disagreed. "As long as he doesn't find out about this charade, you're probably right. And that is by no means a certainty."

"Then you must help me get to Brighton undiscovered. It's more than my happiness relying on it."

He shook his head slowly. "Oh, I think not, my dear. My job is something entirely different now. I only hope in the fullness of time, you'll forgive me for what I'm about to do."

DIANA'S EYES NARROWED, as though she guessed he was about to commandeer her curricle. "Forgive you for what, precisely? In case you hadn't noticed, *I* am the one sitting in this curricle, and *you* are not. So you can't force me to do anything. But pray, do tell, what is your job now?"

To get you back to the man you chose to marry. "To get you back to Sutton and safety. You can't outsmart society. They're too sharp by half."

She raised her chin. "I think I can. I was always good at playing hide-and-seek when we were children. *You* could never find me. I will travel on to Brighton."

He shuddered. "Are we talking about the ammunition chest?"

Just the words "ammunition chest" had the color draining from her face. He wasn't playing fair. "To me, Diana, this is precisely like that day. Pip and I searched for hours, hoping you weren't hurt. Hearing muffled cries but not being able to find you." His chest became tight at the thought, and he took a deep breath. "I'm not a boy now, but if I see you running headlong into danger, I will still do everything in my power to stop you."

She opened her mouth to argue, but he put his hand up to

stop her. "Please don't argue with me. I never again want to experience finding you unconscious inside a wooden box."

She waved away his words with her hand. "Bah. I just exhausted myself crying. I was perfectly able to breathe. There was a crack in the side that let air in."

He closed his eyes and took a deep breath, praying for patience. "You're impossible. I'm trying to help you, and you're making light of it. You're gambling in the worst possible way." There really was no greater insult he could throw at her, if she only knew it. His entire family had crumbled from gambling and the excess that went along with it.

Her back stiffened. "The stakes are too high for me to step away."

"Playing with your past, your family, and your future. Banking on a slim chance. This is a chance for you to do the opposite of what you normally do for once. Why don't you try it and see what happens?"

But the obstinate set of her jaw told him she was in no mood for a lesson. In a man he would have said it was foolhardy, but in her, knowing how society had treated her after her last gamble, it was something akin to suicide.

He closed his eyes and exhaled. Diana was a law unto herself, and the good Lord help him, it was one of the very reasons he loved her.

She leaped forth where his instinct was to withdraw and protect. She was brave, bold, and all the things he had to be if he was going to pull his life out of the depths of despair it was in. He didn't know whether he should encourage it because it was so rare or protect her from the storm that was coming. "What if I carry on to Brighton, in your carriage, so that if you win, the win is yours? I will use the prize money to buy Equinox for my stables if the prince allows it."

It was the end she wanted, without the side plate of ruin.

She paused, deep in thought, then seemed to come to a decision. "Very well." There was a tear in her eye that tugged at his heart and proved once and for all that doing the right thing often felt like the worst thing. Just as it had all those years ago with Fortescue.

Williams tapped him on the shoulder, and he turned to have a brief exchange with him about how to lift Douglas into their curricle without hurting his arm. In the time it took him to have this brief exchange, Diana had called Daniel back to his position behind her. She had the reins in hand and was looking over her shoulder to make sure the road was clear.

His mouth dropped open. "Di— Mr. *Kingsley*!"

He stepped back so she wouldn't drive over his toe. But she just tipped her hat to him like there was no rush. "My thanks, Templeton. I like to make my own decisions. I'm not sure why you thought otherwise." And with that, her horses leapt into action.

"Damn her eyes," Alec said to her retreating form, with nothing left to do but jump in his own curricle and chase after her.

"Her?" Williams said, intrigued. "I *thought* he was a feminine lad."

"Yes 'her,' but if I hear a word of that breathed beyond this roadside, you'll have me to answer to." He strode off before he could say anything else incriminating.

CHAPTER 15

IN WHICH MISS KINGSLEY RECEIVES A BLOW
AND ALEC FIGHTS DIRTY

Diana had no intention of regretting her decision to leave Alec.

And she didn't. At first. At first she'd ridden high in jubilation at the thought that she was making her own decisions. The wind rushed past and suddenly she was in the moment again. Not a spectator but a participant.

After a quick change in Horley without incident, the horses were fresh and ready to chew up the miles to Crawley. There was nothing ahead but a few coaches and a wagon with some pigs jigging around in the back of it. Diana let the two beautiful bays she had hitched up run out their jitters and hoped they would run out her own.

But the truth was that Alec was never the kind to give lectures. He was more likely, as he had back at Kingsley House, to encourage her to wildness and praise her bravery. He had never before brought up that time he found her in the ammunition chest, even though it was one of the most harrowing moments of her life.

After that, enclosed spaces made sweat break out on her neck and the smell of closed-up wood left her short of breath. She didn't like to be locked in, not to anything.

Maybe not even into marriage?

Because Alec was right, she was on a course of action that only the bravest and most liberal of men would forgive her for. Perhaps even her own father would not understand.

So why was she doing it? For Equinox, who had been loyal to her for so long. Once she might have left the task to Father, but by selling her horse, he'd proven himself unworthy. She slackened the reins in thought, and the horses slowed, their ears twitching as they awaited her next command.

What should it be?

To go back or to continue on? Giving up on anything was a horrible thought. She would hate the smug look on Alec's face as she returned to him. She would hate admitting to Pip that she had done the wrong thing. But on the upside, Father need never know she'd raced, and her promise to Cordelia to behave would be kept.

Her shoulders sagged, and her long exhale made her realize just how anxious she'd been.

Daniel was quiet behind her. Not that he was ever exactly verbose. She took a deep breath. "Daniel, I think I shall let you drive the rest of the way to Brighton and take myself back to Sutton at the next change on a horse."

"Very well, Miss Kingsley." There was no surprise in his voice, but definitely a smattering of relief. In her defense, she hadn't thought about how her actions would impact her staff. How Father might see them as responsible for her actions, may question them on their decision not to refuse her service.

Once again, she had put her own self-interest ahead of others in her care. She was a terrible person.

"I do hope my father does not find out about my race," she said.

"He won't hear it from me, Miss Kingsley. I'm glad we're

turning around, and I will be happy to take this curricle to Brighton for you."

"My thanks." She scanned the road ahead. "The next tollgate is less than a half mile ahead. We can turn around there."

Daniel took the yard of tin and kept it by his side. "Good idea." As they drew closer, he lifted the horn to his lips and blared their tune across the countryside.

But the tollgate master did not appear.

Diana frowned. "Try again."

He did, with the same result. Nothing.

Diana shrugged a shoulder. "Well, I suppose it had to fail at some point. Very well, let's do this the old-fashioned way. The ticket for this toll will be in the small black bag at your feet."

A few moments passed as Daniel leafed through all the tickets Diana had purchased the week before. "Here it is."

They slowed at the gate, and Daniel blew the horn again.

What felt like minutes passed with no movement from behind the grimy windows of the tollhouse.

"This is strange. He might just be asleep by the fire. It's been known to happen."

"Let me go and investigate." Daniel took the ticket and opened the door to the tollhouse. He stepped inside and closed the door behind him.

Diana calmed her horses and watched the door. *Hurry up, Daniel.*

The minutes passed and it became apparent she was going to have to go in after him. Which meant putting the horses somewhere safe, not just leaving them standing by the side of the road.

Following the driveway around the side of the tollhouse, she saw a small carriage house and a trough. "There now," she said, leading them to the water and hooking the reins over the post. "I shall be back in just a minute."

It was certainly not ideal for them to be left with their bridles on, but she would only be a moment. Perhaps she might just look through the window and see what was happening.

She turned to do just that when a bag went over her head. But before it did, she glimpsed a monster of a man, built like a pugilist, with a broken nose and scar down his cheek to boot.

Then there was a sharp pain at the back of her head and nothing else.

~

THE SUN GLINTED off Diana's yellow curricle in the distance. She was at the tollgate, which for once did not seem to have opened its gates for her.

"My lord, please sit still I can tie your cravat." Heaven forbid he go with a bare neck for a few miles.

He looked away for a moment as Stephen tied the cravat, and when he looked back, she had disappeared.

"Hell's teeth." His heartbeat thudded in his ears. She should know the dangers at this point. It was foolhardy and reckless.

He encouraged his horses to pick up their pace, then opened them out entirely, letting them gallop along as fast as their legs would carry them, knowing full well that by the time he reached the tollgate, he would have completely blown them. It would not be fair to take them any farther. His race was over, but he couldn't care less.

As he neared the tollgate, he looked around the bend. There was still no sign of Diana. She had completely disappeared. *Stupid. Stupid. Stupid.*

His palms broke out in a sweat, but his mind sharpened, taking in all the details of the surrounding area. Something had happened. She was in trouble. It wasn't just the danger they'd already faced informing him. It was his heart, just knowing, as it had done all those years ago when they played hide-and-seek, telling him he had to find her, and fast.

When he reached the tollgate, the master came out to take his money. He was a huge brute of a man who looked like he'd come straight from Seven Dials, dressed in a linen shirt that might have been white once, and brown leather breeches. "You in the race?"

"Yes, I am in the race. Has a young man in a yellow curricle with red wheels passed through here lately?"

"No," he said flatly, handing him the ticket as though the conversation was over. "This takes you through to Brighton. Good luck to you." He turned the pike to open the gate and motioned for Alec to go through. "Off you go." He ran his hand over the enormous weapon attached to a holster at his waist.

Right. A blunderbuss. Message received.

Alec had a bad feeling he would happily level it at Alec if he questioned him further.

Too bad.

"Sir, with respect, I saw the curricle at a distance, and once it reached your tollgate, it disappeared. Could it be that my friend is here?"

The tollgate master's eyes narrowed. "Many vehicles go through this tollgate. I can't be expected to remember each of them. Now be on your way. You want to win that race? Best go."

Alec did not move his horses. "I will go when it pleases *me*. And it does not please me yet." Nerves for Diana warred with burning-red anger that threatened to overtake him.

The man shrugged. "Suit yourself." He turned and went back into the tollhouse, closing the door firmly.

"He's left the tollgate open!" Stephen said in confusion. The one rule of being the master of a tollgate was that nobody passed it for free.

Alec shook his head. "Stranger and stranger." He took the curricle through the gate. There was a path leading around the back of the tollhouse. Instinct and nothing more told him this was where Diana had gone. He pulled the team over and turned to Stephen. "If you can stay here until I return, do. But if you are in danger, please leave without me."

Keeping himself close to the hedge that bordered the road, he followed the path around to the back of the tollhouse. There, in front of a barn, with the horses still hitched, stood Pip's curricle. Daniel was at the horses' heads, murmuring to them. Horses didn't like to be hitched up too long without moving.

He snuck closer so he could whisper. "Where is Miss Kingsley?"

Daniel turned. His left eye was swollen and red and his lip fat. "She went inside to pay an extra toll," he said. "Our ticket not being the right one and all. I've been instructed to mind the horses." As he said this, his eyes widened and shifted to the side, as though trying to give Alec warning. Alec looked over his shoulder, and behind him in the barn he could see a pistol around the side of the door, trained on the groom.

Alec nodded his understanding. "I'll just be on my way, then," he said loudly. "I was worried he may have lost his purse."

This was very serious indeed. Diana must have been taken inside against her will and was being held there. The back door to the toll house opened and a short, thin man glared around him, pistol in hand. He had taken off his tricorn, revealing that his hair was long around his ears but his head was completely bald.

His gaze narrowed. "Can I help you?"

"This curricle belongs to my friend, Mr. Kingsley. Allow me to introduce myself. I am the Earl of Templeton. Please convey to my friend that I am here to help in any way necessary. Or would you prefer me to fetch the magistrate?"

He crossed his arms over his chest. "Not sure why you'd do that, considering your friend tried to race through the tollgate without paying."

That actually *did* sound like Diana. Perhaps this man did not realize she had prepaid her way to Brighton. "I think you'll find he prepaid his ticket last week. Please bring him to me now. We have been riding this race since nine o'clock this morning and, so far, five accidents have befallen us. Let me assure you, my good friend, the Prince of Wales, will know about each place along his beloved Brighton Road involved in these accidents."

From the front of the tollhouse there was a loud rapport that sounded awfully like gunshot, and then the sound of horses galloping away. Considering there had been nobody close behind him on the road, Alec could only assume the tollgate master had shot his blunderbuss, and his own curricle was now hurtling down the road toward Brighton with Stephen at the reins.

He looked at the man with one eyebrow raised. "That does not sound promising. Bring Mr. Kingsley to me now. You do not want to kidnap the son of one of England's foremost horse breeders. He has friends in higher places than both of us."

A feminine cry punctuated his sentence.

Diana.

"Just my wife," said the man, blinking furiously.

Damnation, enough of this time-wasting. Alec stood back and with none of the finesse that had earned him the moniker *The Velvet Punch* in Gentleman Jackson's boxing salon, he drew the man's cork. He fell to the ground with an awkward thud. "That's better."

There was a muffled cry and he turned to see a man, likely the actual tollgate master, tied up behind the door. He freed him, then ran toward the sound of Diana's voice. It wasn't that hard; the place was tiny. "Please tell me you haven't locked her in something," he said under his breath. "I'll kill you with my bare hands if you've locked her in something." At this point, he'd plow through anyone that stood in his way, magistrate be damned.

Down the hall, a doorknob shook; she was definitely inside whatever room it was. He tried to turn the knob, with no luck. Locked. "Stand back. I'm going to kick the door in."

"There is nowhere for me to go. This is a cupboard." Her voice trembled, taking him straight back to the little girl trapped in the trunk all those years ago.

He turned to see the pretend tollgate master striding down the hall, his spent firearm turned around to serve as a blunt object. Not that he needed it, as his fists were like cannon balls. A bit of dirty fighting would be needed to even up the odds.

If only Gentleman Jackson could see him now.

"One moment, Diana," he said and turned to the man. "I have found my friend, whom I believe has the keys." Alec let his gaze drop to the bunch of keys hanging from the man's belt. "Could you please open the door?"

It was a joke, but nobody laughed.

Instead, the man growled, a deep bellowing noise that did nothing for Alec's nerves and hopes of getting out of this unscathed. The man made a clumsy swing, easily dodged. Sometimes larger men really were awkward.

Alec returned fire with a kick in a place no man wants to be kicked, followed by an elbow to his face as he fell to his knees in agony. Both things he would be ejected from his boxing club for. "Don't tell anyone I did that. Not sporting, you know?"

The man growled and tried to stand up. Alec kicked him back down. He groaned and reached out to trip him.

"That won't do," Alec said and kicked him a little less gently in the solar plexus, then once more and he was unconscious. "Finally," he muttered.

"Alec, are you all right?" The worry in her voice was touching.

"Perfectly fine. I'll have the door open in a trice." It warmed his heart that she thought such a deep and manly groan could come from him.

"I don't suppose there is any rope in that cupboard?"

"Stop talking and get me out of here." He couldn't be annoyed at her demand. There was a horrible edge of desperation in her voice.

With nothing on hand, Alec pulled the cravat from his neck.

"Cravat number two, gone to God. Sad waste of a lovely piece of linen." His valise would have none left at this rate. He pushed the man onto his stomach—no mean feat—and tied him up, then retrieved the key ring and tried each one. None of them fit.

"Hurry, Alec, I can't breathe."

CHAPTER 16

IN WHICH IT IS HARD TO BELIEVE ANYONE EVER CALLED HER LADY LUCK

She couldn't breathe. The familiar panic of being trapped was snaking around her heart and clenching hard. Her body seemed to remember the trauma as though no time had passed.

Enclosed.

Locked in with no means to escape.

It didn't matter that the slimy man had assured her she would be released promptly when one hour had passed. It didn't matter how often she told herself simply to count to one thousand, and it would all be over.

No, her brain was having none of it.

And in her heart she was a five-year-old child, locked in a Chinese ammunition chest when the latch fell shut. Back then, no amount of screaming until she was hoarse had worked, and the terror had mounted until she passed out from it.

She didn't scream now, but only because she was trying so very hard to keep herself calm.

A cupboard is not a chest.

You can do this. What do you have to get out of this scrape?

Hairpins. She found one in her mess of a coiffure and tried to pry open the lock with it.

But it wouldn't budge, and the smell of old wood was a stark reminder of that chest all those years ago—a smell she'd not been able to abide since.

She was trapped, once again, in a box of her own making.

What was her life but one trap after the other? The freedom of girlhood, followed by the bindings of ladyhood, which she tried so hard to escape with her horses. Father, encouraging her to follow through with marriage to a man who did not respect her.

Then spinsterhood with its intricate weave of rules and frustrations. Now she was to marry Colonel Webster and be caught in a lifelong oath from which death was the only escape. Her own choices, made by the only options society gave her.

When was a woman to be free of it? When were they free to live their lives, as a man was free to live his, and make her own decisions?

Even the house she had grown up in was feeling like a prison, with Cordelia putting more and more pressure on her to marry, until finally any passing carriage was a good enough means of escape.

Was that what this race was? Was her eagerness to take up the reins just a reflection on how caged she truly felt? But this race was being taken out of her hands by someone else too. No matter what she did, she was thwarted.

But Alec had found her, just like he had all those years ago. Long after Pip had given up and was eating jam tarts in the nursery, Alec had kept looking room by room until he'd found her in the gunroom, locked in that stupid chest. He'd pulled her out then, and was about to scold her when he saw her tear-streaked face, and instead took her hand and said, "There you are, everything is fine."

He'd then kicked the chest on her behalf and made her laugh when he stubbed his toe.

She rested her head against the cupboard door and smiled at the memory.

Then his voice was in the hallway, and her tears started flowing, as if she'd be holding on to them forever.

It was ugly and hot, and she didn't want to be trapped in this cupboard or her life. The race was a way to escape the choices she'd made, even if it were only for an afternoon, but it was all closing in.

But if she looked closely—had she hoped to be found out? Hoped it would give Colonel Webster a disgust of her?

His footsteps came closer and miraculously a key turned in the lock and the door swung open.

He pulled her into his arms. "Oh, my darling, what an ordeal for you." He held her close and brushed the hair back from where it was stuck to her cheek.

"I was about to save myself with hairpins."

"And you would have, I'm sure. Perhaps I did not have to kick that poor man in the bollocks after all."

She laughed, much the same way she had after he'd stubbed his toe on that chest all those years ago—a mix of relief and happiness. "No, I believe that was the right course of action."

He nodded. "There was no getting past him. He was a mountain of a man. Most ungentlemanly of me." He cupped her face in his hands. She had lost her hat, and her hair spilled over her shoulders. He pulled his handkerchief from his pocket and gently dabbed her face. "Everything is fine. Let's find your hat."

"Don't leave me."

He went to the cupboard and fetched it out; then he placed it on her head. "I have no intention of leaving, and, in any case, I believe Stephen has inadvertently taken off with my curricle. Did you hear the blunderbuss? I believe that was your abductor encouraging him to move on."

Her hands were clammy and she rubbed them down her breeches. "How will we get out of here?"

"I found the real tollgate master tied up behind the door. He will have taken things in hand. But stay behind me."

She lowered her voice to a whisper. "I never knew how heroic you were." *How right it feels to depend on you.*

"And I have never been so relieved to find someone in my life. It has taken every ounce of will I have not to be very *unheroic* and kiss you."

A wave of longing hit her. Her legs felt heavy, her knees weak. "Don't let me stop you."

It had been many years since her last kiss and she could think of no one she'd like to kiss more than Alec. Just this once, before the trap was well and truly sprung. "And don't hold back."

"Damn me," he said softly and pulled her to him.

Her hat fell off the back of her head again, and he took advantage of it by running his fingers in her hair, setting her senses alight. His lightest touch creating a swirl of reactions inside her.

Templeton.

Alec.

Touching her like she was the most precious thing. Then he brought his mouth down to hers as though he'd been waiting an entire lifetime to kiss her and wasn't about to get it wrong. As though he'd been dreaming of this moment forever.

Diana closed her eyes and surrendered to the heat of his lips, the taste of him and the warmth that spread from her lips down to her toes. It felt like falling through dark warm space with Alec as her guiding star. As he always seemed to be.

Her legs weakened beneath her, so she leaned against the wall. That was better anyway, because he moved his hands from her hair to slide them down her arms and around her waist. Templeton. Kissing her.

The race was worth it just for this.

"My dear love," he whispered next to her mouth. She shivered, then stopped him from saying more by taking his lips again.

She was his dear love? What was this madness? She had spent years pining for him, waiting for him, but his tone suggested *he'd* waited a very long time to kiss *her*.

This time she was braver, cupping either side of his face with her hands, tasting him, craving him. It was a hunger she would never assuage, and if they weren't in the cramped hall of a tollhouse, she would do this all afternoon. Devil take the race and all its craziness. If this was why people married, now, she finally understood.

Eventually, she pulled away to catch her breath, feeling dazed and a little drunk.

He pulled her close to him. His heart beat hard through his linen shirt, but not nearly as hard as hers. "My goodness. I know I said 'don't hold back', but ..."

Opening her eyes was like awakening from a dream. The world they built inside that kiss was heaven, and it was taking some time for her to return to earth. And maybe she didn't want to. Her lips tingled and heat roared through her.

Their gazes connected, and he tilted his head so their foreheads rested together. He exhaled a shuddering breath. "I have been holding back for too long. Now my dream has come to life."

But that was all it was. A dream. Her whole body stilled and she closed her eyes. How very Diana Kingsley to discover the man of her dreams loved her, when she'd given up hope and become engaged. She'd already jilted one man. She'd suffered and her life had changed for the worse because of it. Her family's life had changed because of it. It was one thing to go your own merry way and be happy with the consequences, but when the ones you loved suffered, well, it made a person pause.

How could she possibly do it again? It might be a bitter thing to swallow, but she must forget this ever happened. Because nothing would come of it. Ever. And she couldn't let Alec think that it could. Not that he would. How long had she been waiting for him to notice her, to offer for her and *now* he chooses to declare himself. If she didn't want to kiss him again so badly she could slap him.

He took her hand. "Come. Let's get out of this place."

As they walked down the corridor, she had to step over the hulk of a man who had put the bag on her head. He stirred as they came closer, so she leaned down and twisted his ear. "I'm only sad I didn't get to draw your cork myself."

Alec rolled his eyes. "Trust me, he has been well punished, my dear. And the law will do the rest." He held out his hand for her to take.

It felt so right. As right as she knew it would. She shook her head at her own stupidity. It was hard to believe anyone had ever called her Lady Luck.

CHAPTER 17

HOPING FOR THE BEST, TEMPLETON CONFIDES THE WORST

His legs still shaky after the most awe-inspiring kiss of his life, Alec walked into the middle of the Brighton Road and looked south. There was no sign of his curricle.

But that was no surprise. He would not expect Stephen to wait around when people were shooting at him.

He turned to Diana. "May I ride with you to Brighton?" *Can we sit side by side? Will you let me see you safe? Maybe forever?* Her heart was his, not Colonel Webster's, and now that he knew that, he was ready to fight.

Throwing caution to the wind felt like the perfect choice. Certainly, there was the small issue of her engagement to Colonel Webster. But surely they could weather the storm together? She had to see it was worth it. Or he had to convince her of it before they reached Brighton and the weight of her family's expectations bore down on her.

She nodded, a little too perfunctory for his liking. "Of course. Where is Daniel? I hope he is unharmed." She frowned, looking around for her groom. "This race has been a disaster from the moment it began."

Bright curls sprang out from under her hat in a most becoming way. "You're not wrong there. Worst hundred guineas I ever spent." *Best hundred guineas I ever spent.*

She nodded. "I should never have done it."

He couldn't say the same when the outcome had meant kissing her. His lips still tingled as he relived it over and over. He reached for her hand. *You waited too long, Alec my boy. But it's not too late.* "But if you had never done it, would we be standing where we are right now?"

Her brows drew together, but she didn't let go. "What, staring up the road, looking for a missing curricle with no chance of winning the race or getting my horse back?"

"It's an adventure and somewhat fun, admit it."

She shook her head, smiling in disbelief. "Only you would call it fun to be shot at, held at gunpoint, kidnapped, and locked in a cupboard."

He winced. When she said it like that … "Maybe it proves that anything I do with you is the best time of my life. Yes, we've lost the race, but if it means we found each other, I regret nothing."

She tilted her head and if he had to guess, he would say she was annoyed, which made no sense. "Well, *I* regret it. Do you know how it feels to wait for you to notice me these past, oh I don't know, *ten years*." She pursed her mouth. "And now that I am engaged, you decide to notice. It is *beyond* vexing. I could box your ears." Movement next to the tollhouse caught her attention. "Ah, there he is."

His head spun and he dropped her hand. What happened to *she thinks of you as a brother*? "Did you say you have been waiting for me for ten years? So before Fortescue?" His mind could not comprehend it.

She ignored him as Daniel emerged from behind the tollhouse, leading the horses that were hitched up to the Kingsley curricle. "Miss Kingsley, thank the lord. I don't mind telling you that hearing that gun go off scared me half to death."

"But Daniel, your face! What did they do to you?"

Daniel lifted his chin. "Better to ask what I did to *them*. I handled myself."

"Of course you did." Diana went to the horses' heads and gave them each a few dates from her pocket. "Thank you, Daniel. I am very glad to be in one piece and see you are in one piece as well." Her voice was level, but her cheeks were flushed a fiery red.

"These two are ready." Daniel turned to Alec and nodded. "Is Lord Templeton taking my place in the curricle? One of Kingsley's grooms will return through here soon enough with a horse for me to carry on to Brighton. That is, I assume you will want to travel with him to Brighton rather than back to Sutton? Mr. Kingsley is there."

Diana climbed into the driver's seat and took the reins. "Yes. Good idea. Next time you tell me something is not right, I daresay I will listen! You are worth your weight in gold, Daniel." She handed him Pip's purse. "Take this in case you need it."

Alec jumped into the seat next to Diana, keeping his silence. *Ten years.* When she discovered his circumstances, she might not want to marry him, but that seemed beside the point right now.

She looked over her shoulder and launched the horses onto the road. He allowed her a few minutes to run out their jitters and then turned to her. "Miss Kingsley. Do not pretend you have been waiting for me to notice you for ten years, when in that time you have been engaged to Fortescue and now Webster."

Both eyebrows lifted. "*Only* because you never offered and were never *going* to offer." She cut him off with a stern stare. "Not after I debuted, or jilted Fortescue, or, oh, any of the number of times you could have! You never courted me, Alec. You flirt, you dance divinely, and nothing ever comes of it."

Nothing ever comes of it? He closed his eyes and took a deep breath against the pain her words brought. "Nothing ever comes of it for two reasons. Would you like to know what they are?"

She arched an eyebrow. "Certainly. If you think you can

explain away a decade of inaction, I am all ears." Her voice was wobbly, suggesting she had more at stake than she'd like to let him know.

"Very well," he said urbanely and felt the small tick start in his clenched jaw. He did not want to share this story only to have her look at him with pity. "Then let me tell you. And if you decide you would like to marry me in the future, well, you will be in possession of all the facts."

"Do tell." She tilted her face toward him, no longer looking annoyed, just curious.

Even Pip had not heard the entirety of it. Nobody, not even the members of his club, Wrack and Ruin, knew it all. But if there was anyone he wanted to understand, it was Diana. That she should think he had been indifferent to her all these years was much worse than losing his pride.

"You know my father died just over two years ago. But he did not die in a riding *accident* as so many think he did." He took a deep breath. How did you word something so heartbreaking? "He was riding, but it was entirely deliberate. When he finally comprehended what his lifestyle had done to our wealth, he couldn't face it. He …"

"Oh, Alec, say no more." He turned to see that her warm, caramel eyes were brimming with tears. "Your poor father."

Strangely, none of the anger he usually felt toward his father was there. "Our assets were gone, our debts insurmountable. The only thing he did right was dying in something that looked like an accident so the law did not get involved. I've been dealing with the complete disintegration of the estate, and it would be a knave's job to offer for any lady when all I have is debt and the futile hope I can turn it around."

She drew in a shocked breath. "But how terrible!"

He nodded, unable to meet her gaze and see the pity there. "I'm fighting, though. Trying to improve the productivity of the lands, reducing costs wherever I can. I've managed to keep all the staff, although not the ones who were part of the problem. I spent months poring over the books, trying to make sense of where the money went."

"And where did it go?"

He shrugged. He was angry for so long, but it no longer mattered where it went, only that it was gone. "Chiefly gambling, excessive spending, and the Prince of Wales."

She kept her eyes on the road, but her eyebrows furrowed. "What has Prinny to do with it? Other than encouraging excess in all its forms, that is."

"A heap of IOUs that I found in my father's desk amounting to over one hundred and fifty thousand pounds."

"Oh, my." Manners forgotten, her mouth fell open, reins slackened in her hand. He pulled her hands up again, so the horses weren't confused.

Well might she be shocked. It was the kind of money that should have fueled generations of Templeton earls. Instead, it probably purchased a few statues, a snuffbox, and some marble floor. "And he will not enter into correspondence. All polite enquiry has been ignored."

"And to think we sold him Equinox!" There was a patch of bright red on her cheeks, and her mouth was pursed. "I wonder if he actually paid?"

"Who knows? *I* wonder how he can keep spending when he owes so many people so much money. But there you have it." He kept his voice even, hoping he did not leach his longing for her into it. "So, I have always considered myself a poor bargain. You would indeed be much better off with Colonel Webster, if you want to eat and be clothed, that is." He laughed ruefully.

She stayed silent as she overtook a coach with her usual expert ease and for the minute after as she regulated the team's pace. Then she turned to him. "And the second reason?"

He smiled, as though it would soften the blow. "Your father told me not to. More than once. The last time I tried, he said he had asked you and that you said you viewed me as more of a brother. He's always been very polite about it."

"You did? He did?" She seemed to choke up. "Oh." He looked at her to see that while she still held perfect form, her back straight and shoulders back, tears were pouring down her face. The tip of her nose had turned red and she hiccupped.

He put his arm around her shoulder. "I'm sorry. And the way you always teased me just as you did Pip, I began to believe that was the only way you saw me too. Would you like me to take the reins?"

She nodded and pulled a handkerchief from her pocket, dabbing it under her eyes. "I shall kill him."

Templeton nodded. "I think after Fortescue, he was just being careful. How could he be sure that I wasn't just trying to repair my situation with your dowry?"

She reached over and took the reins back. "Because he has known you since you were a child, that's how. It would serve him right if we eloped."

But there was something in her voice that told him that was the last thing she was going to do. "I would drive this contraption all the way to Scotland, if I thought you would. In case you have not realized it yet, I am hopelessly in love with you. Your courage, strength, and intelligence are the standard to which all other women are compared. And all of them fail miserably, because they are not you. I even find your tempers charming."

It only made her cry again. *Excellent work, Alec, dear chap.* "We cannot. I cannot." Her shoulders shuddered. "It's not possible. Not now." She took a deep, unsteady breath. "No, let us stop this talk. If I entertain it, I will go mad." She had allowed the horses to pick up their pace even more, and now they were ripping through the countryside.

They drove for a mile or so, with Diana just talking to her horses rather than him. "Steady on there," she cooed over and over, and he wasn't sure if she was telling the horses to settle or herself. Her soft, lilting voice had the horses in an even, steady pace within a few minutes.

Then Alec broke.

"Do you truly not want to talk about it? Because I will not force my attentions on you. I will not ask you to marry me, if you don't want me to."

She looked straight ahead at the road. "I think I would prefer, at the moment, if you did not." She shot him a glance and a quick smile.

He let the words sink in. *At the moment.*

THEY DROVE ON IN SILENCE, Diana thinking furiously. This was Templeton. He didn't deserve that she should withhold anything from him. Especially not when she knew what it must have cost him to admit the truth of his situation and of how he felt about her. He who all the ton thought still rolled in excess. Her cheeks reddened when she remembered how she'd accused him of gambling just a few weeks ago. Nothing could have been further from the truth. And to deal with that on top of the death of his father and keeping it all to himself. It made her heart feel like a heavy thing.

The change at Pease Pottage came into view, and all conversation halted as the Kingsley grooms stepped forward to change the horses. Diana and Alec drank from their flasks, rather than the refreshment offered to them by the publican of the Black Swan.

"Would you like to drive this stage?" Diana said. Not that she couldn't drive, but it would be nice to take a rest, especially since the road was about to traverse the St. Leonard's Forest area of Sussex. She always found the dappled sunlight difficult to drive through.

"I should be delighted," Alec said, for all the world like they had not spoken of marriage and debt and how much he loved her. That was the gentleman he was. He would never put her to the blush or pressure her for an answer, and no matter what his feelings, he would always be her friend, before anything else.

Soon enough, tall trees surrounded them, and the countryside turned from lush rolling green hills to the sort of forest one would expect medieval bandits to emerge from. Birdsong drifted down from the bowers, and the forest floor was layered with ferns.

It smelled damp.

She looked across at Alec, who managed her team with a gentle but firm hand. His profile showed his firm jaw with the beginnings of a shadow that she'd felt when he kissed her. His dark hair curled around his shirt points. There was a smudge of mud high on his cheekbone she wanted to brush away. He'd abandoned his great coat and was riding in just his shirt and a burgundy silk vest, without a cravat. Even worn down by the road and their adventures, he still made her heart clutch. "You have lost your cravat again."

He turned to her and gave her a crooked smile. "My first one went to Douglas, the second to that brute at the tollhouse. But Jenkins packs me at least ten, for we all know what a perfectionist I am." He looked around him. "What a pretty part of the world this is."

She ignored the proffered polite conversation. "Just so you know, I would love nothing better than to marry you, rich or poor. But, I am betrothed. I should not have even kissed you."

He groaned. "Please tell me you do not regret it. For if this road weren't so narrow, I would pull us to the side and do it all again." His countenance darkened. "Betrothals can be broken. I would run the gauntlet of society damning us, if it meant you were by my side."

"And if it were only you and I to worry about, so would I. But

I have a duty to my family. You know what happened last time. What of Pip? What of Father?"

He nodded and threw her a glance that told her he could see. All too well. He understood her family and how important their business was. They didn't have a thousand acres of land that formed the basis of their wealth. They had their horses and the goodwill of the people who purchased them.

"And it was easy when it was Fortescue," she continued, "because he ridiculed me. It boded badly for the future. But Colonel Webster is a good man. He esteems me highly, and he wants to marry me for more than just my inheritance. I think." Alec tried to interrupt, but she put her hand up.

"Yes, yes, I know that you would offer for me, too, especially after what we have endured together today; however, I don't know how I am to remove myself from this situation and not bring shame on both myself and my family. In fact, even just thinking about it makes me feel ill."

"Ill enough to give your entire life to a man you don't love? For you don't love him, do you?"

She looked up, knowing the answer to his question would be in her eyes. "If you can find me a way out that doesn't bring shame on me, my family, or Colonel Webster … if we can find a quiet way, then it would make me the happiest creature in the world to marry you."

She hardly dared to let herself hope. Surely it was too late; the die was cast and not in Lady Luck's favor.

"Because we both know that is what you want to do," Alec said, giving her a cheeky grin in an attempt to lift her spirits.

She took a deep breath, wishing she could capture this moment, and his grin, in a painting so it would last forever. "I can't deny it," she said. "You have ever charmed me."

He reached over and touched her cheek. "That is the nicest thing you have ever said to me. Although, considering you spend half your time finding ways to poke at me, this is not surprising …"

"I never meant any of it," she whispered.

He threaded the reins through one hand and reached for her hand with the other.

They made their way through the Sussex countryside, the road winding around woodland areas and crossing over streams on their way to the river Adur. "Then let's enjoy this day, and let's enjoy this ride into Brighton, as though I have already fixed all of our problems. Because I assure you I will. I've come up against enough of life's tragedies to know what I'm made of. I may have lost almost all my riches, but if I lose you I will finally be poor."

Diana shimmied herself to be even closer to him on the narrow seat and rested her head on his shoulder. "In that case, I have plenty of ideas for what we can do with my dowry to build the most amazing horse breeding program England has ever seen." Because if there was one thing Alec never did, it was put her in a "she's just a lady" box. They would always discuss their way forward and take an equal role in decisions. All the changes he'd made to his curricle for the race on her advice were proof of that. He took her seriously.

But there was no hope. She knew it even as she entered into the plans with him. They were dreams spun of the lightest spider web and would blow away in a strong breeze.

CHAPTER 18

IN WHICH A GOOD CHAT IS HAD

Alec was almost glad to see the quaint village of Preston Park, for it meant Brighton was close and this blasted race would be over. Then he could start on the even bigger challenge of extricating Diana from her betrothal. Somehow with no repercussions for anyone involved.

He understood, but couldn't help the feeling that the world would conspire against them and that he would once again be standing in St. George's chapel for her marriage. Not to him.

Diana spent the last leg to Brighton with her head resting on his shoulder and her hand firmly clasped in his. Almost like she thought this was the first and last time she would be able to.

"Here we are," he said as the team passed through the last turnpike of the race, with no criminals evident.

She raised her head and looked around. "That was way too fast."

The traffic had built up again, and they had to wait their turn as a stagecoach and a wagon with chairs piled on the back lined up, too, but soon enough the outskirts of Brighton came into view.

The horses seemed happy for the slower pace of the

metropolis. Diana spent a few moments telling them what splendid horses they were. *Oh to be a horse in the care of her.*

Alec turned to her. "How would you like to play this, my love?" There was no way he was going to stop calling her that in private. If he failed and she went ahead with her marriage, he had to take it while he could.

A flush of red appeared on her cheeks, and a small smile tugged on her mouth. "I don't want to be in the curricle when it arrives at the marine pavilion with all those people."

"No, indeed."

"I will make my way to Uncle Horatio's on Ship Street. If you let me alight a little before that, I can simply walk down."

"That does sound simple." If there was one thing about Diana, nothing was ever simple. "But I would much rather drop you at your uncle's door."

"But it is past the finish line. What good would that do?"

He laughed. "I'm quite sure we have not won the race."

"You don't know that, and until you do, you are racing in Pip's curricle, and I want you to take it to the finish." She raised her chin in the air, as though daring him to deny her.

As if he would.

"As you wish." She would probably watch him all the way down the Steine to make sure he didn't double back to ensure she arrived safely. Well, Brighton was not a den of iniquity. She would make it to her uncle's house unharmed.

The London road turned into the North Steine Parade, and the finish line was almost within view.

"Look at the crowd!"

People were lining both sides of the road with the crowds thickening closer to the pavilion. "Best you alight," Alec said, gently guiding the team to the side of the road.

Diana jumped down and unhitched her valise from the back. Then, she returned and offered him her hand, as a gentleman would. "Thank you, my dear Templeton. If nothing else comes of this race, you were right, we found each other and it was the most fun I have had in an age." She dashed a tear away from her cheek. "Now go and finish this debacle."

They were good tears, right? He could never tell. All he wanted was for her to be happy, and any kind of tears at all would contradict that. "I will see you soon." He hoped the look he gave her was enough of a promise to keep her strong until he could fix the mess they found themselves in.

He checked the traffic and eased the curricle back onto the road, picking up speed until the marine pavilion was within sight, instantly wishing Diana was still with him. "Will you look at that?"

The giant dome of the new stables dwarfed the subtle classical lines of the prince's marine pavilion, looking like an Indian palace rising on the Brighton skyline. It only got bigger and more impressive as he drew closer. *Good lord, what was Prinny thinking?* That dome belonged in Constantinople or Bombay, not in staid old Brighton. Knowing the prince, he would use the new architecture of the stables to rebuild the pavilion itself to match. No expense spared.

He pulled his eyes back to the road. People lined the side of the Steine and were cheering and waving as he passed. The lines of crowd showed him where to lead his horses, to drive through the gates and into the gardens. He ran a hand through his hair and put his hat back on.

The timekeeper stood next to a table, flanked by a group of the prince's hussars in their navy uniforms, gold braiding shining in the sun. The white feathers on their hats fluttered in the breeze. He drew his horses up to a gliding stop Diana would be proud of.

"Your number!" the timekeeper said.

"Kingsley entry number eight," Alec replied.

The timekeeper blinked in confusion. "You are Lord Templeton, though. Where is Mr. Philip Kingsley?"

"Injured on the road. My understanding is that it is the vehicle that is entered in the race rather than the driver and that two drivers are allowed."

"True, true. You are only the second vehicle to arrive."

One of the hussars yelled, "Hush, I can't hear" and all at once, the rest of the crowd decided they might like to hear, too, and an unnatural quiet descended.

Alec addressed the crowd. "Many entrants have met with foul play along the road. Pip Kingsley had a branch fall on his head and did not make it past Sutton, where he is recovering. Entrants two through five were waylaid by criminals and tied to trees. I released them and they should be behind me. I have no idea what happened to entrant seven. Beau Kingsley's grooms were drugged at The Old Angel in Woodhatch, while my curricle and groom were shot at by persons who had commandeered the tollhouse before Crawley. That I stand here at all is a miracle, and if I have won, I win for Beau Kingsley. Although I am not sure how, under the circumstances, anyone can be named the winner. A more unfair race I have never run!"

He looked around the crowd and spotted Diana's father, his face stricken.

Alec got down from the curricle, two of the hussars coming forward to take the horses' heads. "We'll take these two around to the stables, my lord."

"My thanks," he said, signing the form proffered by the time-keeper with a flourish. He scanned the sheet. Malmsbury had arrived almost two hours previously, meaning he was likely the clear winner. If there was such a thing.

Beau Kingsley threaded his way through the crowd, his hand outstretched for Alec to shake. "Is Pip injured?"

"We have much to discuss, and this is far too public a place to do it."

Diana's father nodded. "Come, let me show you the stables.

The prince has limited access to them before the grand opening, so we should have some privacy."

Following Beau Kingsley into the stables was a lesson in social niceties. Everyone from the hussars to grooms to members of the peerage nodded or greeted him as he passed. He even made agreements for people to visit the stud. His place in society had been reestablished, that much was certain. No wonder Diana was reluctant to invite scandal into their lives.

Alec looked around. There was an air of excitement and wonder at the new stables that did not reflect the trauma he had just been through.

"Tell me everything," Mr. Kingsley said. "Was he conscious?"

It was apparent he had not put together the fact that Alec left before Pip and had no idea that Diana had ridden. Alec intended to keep it that way.

"Concussed but alert. We left him at The Cock."

His eyes narrowed. "We?"

Alec rolled his eyes at his own stupidity. He'd kept his vow for all of one second.

It was at that moment they came upon the new domed stable, and Alec ignored the question as he gawked at his surroundings.

This was what the prince spent *his* blunt on?

Built like a maharajah's palace, the main building was a circular room with an eighty-foot dome, whose roof seemed to be made entirely of glass. The fluted windows were so clear it felt like one could touch the clouds that rolled across the sky above them. Golden walls bathed the horses in soft light, and there were so many doors and windows it would be impossible to know which one you should go in.

It had two levels. The second level, perhaps housing staff, was a stretch of ornate Indian-styled balconies, so spectators could look down on proceedings on the stable floor.

But Beau Kingsley was not transfixed. He stared at Alec with a flinty eye. "Where, pray tell, is Diana? And do not tell me she is in

Sutton with Pip. I'm not a fool. I will discover the truth so you might as well tell me."

He certainly was not a fool. But then Diana had inherited that sharp brain from somewhere.

Equinox was in a king-sized stall on the other side of the stables. Alec would know that beautiful brute anywhere. He could also see Honey, the pony, standing next to him. Mr. Kingsley made toward them.

"You will find Diana at Uncle Horatio's on Ship Street."

Mr. Kingsley turned to him. "God's teeth, Templeton. Could you not stop her?" His tone was hushed but angry.

Alec's grip on his own anger loosened. "I think you'll find not a hair on her head out of place," he replied.

"And *I* think you should have turned her around the moment you discovered she was driving and got her back to the first stage," her father countered, opening the door to Equinox's stall. "Because now that I think about it, you left before Pip, did you not? You were not at Sutton to see if he was unconscious or otherwise, which meant that Diana drove for him and some-where along the road passed you. Not that I am surprised." He let out a bitter laugh.

"I suppose that means you have never tried to get your daughter to do something that she truly does not want to do?" Alec said, swallowing his annoyance. "Because I assure you nothing I said convinced her, and I was faced with the prospect of either turning back or riding along with her to ensure her safety. I can't believe I need to explain this to you."

Beau had the grace to look chagrined. "She can be somewhat headstrong. Can I assume that nothing untoward happened between you both on the road?"

Alec stepped into the stall, picked up a brush, and gave his attention to Honey. He had a soft spot for the pony who was the love of Equinox's life. He looked up from brushing her mane and regarded the older man with good humor. "What would you deem untoward? For you know that I have loved your daughter since I first laid eyes on her."

Mr. Kingsley's mouth pursed into an unhappy frown. "You know better than to pursue that. My thoughts on this have not changed. You have shown no ability to do anything to stem the losses that your father created."

And here he had thought he'd kept the family debt a well-guarded secret. Well, at least it confirmed why Beau had turned him down so many times. Damn English politeness. He could have saved himself a lot of pointless shuffling if only he'd known. "I am not my father." Although it certainly felt like he was being haunted by him from the grave.

"I know you are not the man he was; however, some legacies last generations, and I fear his is one of those." Beau gave his full attention to Alec. "I will tell you now what I told you five years ago, and again two years ago. You cannot marry her. But this time, not because of your situation, but because she is engaged. Egad, Templeton, she could not cry off, not even if she wanted to."

"No, and I can assure you she does not want to. She thinks it is her *duty* to marry this man, to remove herself from Kingsley House and to redeem herself for Fortescue all those years ago. As if it was *her* fault he was a fool."

Mr. Kingsley frowned. "You're wrong. She wants to marry Webster. And please, if you love her, don't get in the way of it. If she jilts him, her reputation and ours along with it will be ruined beyond redemption. If that happens, I could never forgive such a gross betrayal."

All that was clear enough and in every way exactly what Alec had expected. Certainly, he had hoped that, after hearing of his actions on the road and how he took care of his daughter, that Mr. Kingsley may have seen that Diana would be best off with a man who loved her more than anything. But that was just a ridiculous idea.

"Come now. You are a *good* man. Trying to steal Diana from her fiancé is not the act of a gentleman. It is the act of a fortune hunter."

How dare he? "Careful, Mr. Kingsley. You know me better than that." It was the kind of insult that men called each other out for last century. It hurt like Kingsley had punched him without warning.

Beau must have seen the red light in Alec's eyes. He raised his hand in supplication. "You're right, I do. But I still don't want my hard work poured into your spendthrift father's estate."

Now was not the time to be insulted. His mind whirred with the arguments he could use to bring Mr. Kingsley around. Heaven knew they needed someone on their side. "Or, you could say, that you will be investing in your grandchild, who will have your wealth and my title. But if that's what you think, with all my heart, I would beg you to *disinherit her*. Problem solved. I couldn't care if she never saw another penny from your estate."

Beau searched Alec's face. "And that is the problem, for if you don't marry well, how are you to give your family the life it deserves? I know your pockets are to let and that you have debt all over town. Certainly not your debt, but debt nevertheless. So how, with a legacy that is three-quarters debt and one-quarter assets that you can't access, can you turn things around?"

"I can, and I will. You underestimate me."

"No, actually, I don't. That's why I am putting aside my scruples to warn you off. I know you were at the heart of her break up with Fortescue."

Mr. Kingsley stopped talking as two men walked past the stall and greeted them. He exchanged pleasantries for a few minutes about Equinox and the stables, as if he wasn't embroiled in a heated conversation. The gentlemen did not notice the rising flush of red above his shirt collar. They moved on, and Mr. Kingsley turned back to him. "She could've been a *countess*."

He huffed out a breath. "She would be a countess if she married *me*."

Mr. Kingsley picked up Equinox's reins and led him out of the stall toward the magnificent horse trough in the center of the dome. "How did your father lose his fortune in any case? Did you figure out where it went?"

Alec followed with Honey, not wanting her to miss out. "It likely went to build this—he loaned the prince so much that he could never pay it back out of his allowance. It would take an act of parliament to get it back. I have a better solicitor now; there is hope."

Mr. Kingsley waved him off. "Maybe. You need an heiress, but not my daughter. Now, let's stop talking about this. I wish I had never put voice to it."

Alec took a breath, his mind reeling from Mr. Kingsley's true feelings. "That was some plain talking. I suppose I will never sample Kingsley hospitality again."

If Diana needed him to do this with her family's blessing, as well as not to bring shame on them, things just got a lot harder. Worse still, perhaps he really wasn't the best man for her, as much as his heart told him he was.

All the elation he felt on their drive into Brighton evaporated. He should have known better than to hope. What right did he have to the likes of Diana Kingsley? A woman with grace, courage, beauty and intelligence. None at all. But he also wasn't going to let Beau Kingsley know he'd been dealt a blow.

"We'll come around in time. After she is safely married. That is my only focus."

"Well then, best of luck marrying her to a man who is going to make her supremely unhappy. I'm glad to see you have her best interests at heart."

Mr. Kingsley looked at him steadily. "Yes, I do. And to that end, I must go to Ship Street now." He did not extend his hand for Alec to shake, and Alec didn't offer his. Instead, they gave each other a curt nod that spoke volumes. Beau reached out his hand. "I'll take Honey back."

Alec handed him the reins.

"Excellent chat," Alec said to Mr. Kingsley's departing form. He looked across the stable to see Captain Malmsbury surrounded by a posse of his fellow hussars. There was an air of jubilation that was entirely annoying. He strode across the stable floor. That man had better have a good reason for sailing through the race when everyone else had floundered.

He wasn't in the mood for lies.

CHAPTER 19

IN WHICH MISS KINGSLEY'S RUN OF (ILL) LUCK CONTINUES

It was unfortunate that Cordelia was preparing to leave Uncle Horatio's house at the very moment Diana lifted her hand to the door knocker.

Cordelia had her parasol in one hand, and it dropped to the floor. The look on her face would have been priceless if Diana had not known what was going to follow it.

"Diana?" Her voice was faint, and the color leached from her cheeks. "Quickly, Hatch, close the door."

Diana put both hands up, hoping to calm the oncoming storm. "Nobody saw me alight from the vehicle, and Templeton took it to the finish line."

Cordelia stiffened, and then she shook her head. "Dear Lord, you were in the race? Why are you dressed thus? Where is Pip?"

It was a lot of questions, but she didn't seem to expect any answers. "No one must see you until you change." She looked at the butler. "Fetch a maid to attend Miss Kingsley." She looked Diana up and down. Her voice was grim. "You're filthy! I hope we can salvage whatever you have done, or I won't be responsible for the outcome! Meet me in the sitting room when you look like a lady again." With that, she left the room, leaving Diana holding her valise in the entry.

Hatch picked up the parasol and leaned it up against the wall. He looked at Diana and smiled. "It looks to old Hatch as though Miss Diana has been up to her usual tricks." He shook his head ruefully. "Devil to pay this time, I think, miss!"

Diana shrugged her shoulders. "Five minutes later and she would have been out of the house and none the wiser! Thus is my luck today."

Would it be too much to ask that she could have a few minutes alone to digest everything she'd learned today? At some point she had to just stop and sit with it to clear her mind and try to find the best course of action.

With the help of the maid, Diana was washed and dressed in fresh clothes Cordelia had brought along for her. She made her way down to the sitting room. Cordelia sat staring out the window at the small side garden. Birds fluttered in a birdbath and the late-summer salvias still bore some bright-pink blooms.

Cordelia turned, her face pinched. "I suppose you think that was a great lark."

Diana took a seat, determined to hold her own. She was of age, and could make her own decisions without the input of anyone. "Lark? No indeed, it has been a disaster from the beginning." If Cordelia wanted to have an honest conversation, she stood ready for it.

"Expect the disaster to continue because we have been invited to the ball tomorrow and if you managed to escape notice today, I will be most astounded. Nobody there will think it amusing, I assure you!"

Diana exhaled and closed her eyes. *Oh, that I could be anywhere else.* The front door opened, words were murmured and footsteps sounded down the hall.

Cordelia lifted her chin. "Did Templeton goad you on? That man never has your best interests at heart. Do not deny it."

"Indeed, I do deny it."

Father burst into the room, his eyes wild before they landed on Diana. "What do you deny?" Father's eyes narrowed. "That you raced? For I know that to be true."

She smoothed her skirts. "No, I deny Templeton encouraged me. Nothing could be further from the truth." She counted off on her fingers. "First, he pleaded with me to turn back to the first stage and return to Beth and Pip, several times. Second, when he could no longer do that, he threw his own race, the winnings of which I believe he may desperately need, so that he could protect me. Even then I refused to drive with him, only to result in my being kidnapped and placed in a cupboard. Nothing he said or did could make me turn around and not finish this race. Indeed, I would still be locked in a cupboard just outside of Crawley if he had not taken his protective duties so seriously. Papa, he did not compromise me, he protected and saved me."

"From your own folly, perhaps," Father said. Then her words seemed to sink in. "Did you say you were kidnapped? By Jove he did a bad job of protecting you, didn't he?"

Diana slumped in her chair. Why could they not, for once, support her? Even when she was wrong? It was exhausting. "You know, Papa, there was nothing stopping me from entering this race. You know as well as I do the rules did not stipulate that one had to be a gentleman, and that the race was open to ladies."

"But your reputation is so fragile. How could you expose yourself to that kind of censure?" He ran a hand through his silver hair. "I only hate to think what Colonel Webster will think if he finds out what you have done."

Her stomach fell. "He is not coming to Brighton, is he?" She didn't want to see him while she was dreaming of ways to end their engagement. The thought made her squirm.

Cordelia brushed down her skirts as though flicking away dirt would flick the problem of Diana away with it. "He will be at the ball tomorrow night, and I expect you to deny at every turn the fact that you raced. We may yet get out of this."

Their disapproval was everything she'd tried to avoid, but incurred anyway. Diana took a deep breath and exhaled. "I seem to do nothing but make you both ashamed of me. I wonder why you bother sometimes."

Father raised his eyebrows as though she had surprised him. "It is my job to ensure you are taken care of, not just for now, but after I am gone." And once again the implication that she was incapable of taking care of herself fell over Diana like a wet blanket. With her inheritance, she shouldn't actually need a husband unless she wanted one, but it seemed nobody would trust her to be in charge of her own future.

"Is that why you refused Templeton when he asked to court me? Because you didn't think he could *take care of me*? I have enough to take care of both of us, forever. How could you?"

He crossed his arms over his chest. "I will see you settled to a man who can take just as good care of you as I do." He looked to Cordelia for reassurance, and she nodded.

She thought of the way Templeton fought for her and pulled her out of the closet, cupping her face in his hands as he inspected her to make sure she sustained no injury. "But care is more than money in my purse. A man who loves me for who I am, not who he would like me to be, is worth more than all the gold in my dowry."

Father shook his head sadly. "When one is young, one thinks that way. Trust me, the man who can provide for you and your future family is Colonel Webster."

"He holds you in the highest esteem, my dear!" Cordelia interjected, reaching her hand out to touch Diana. "How could you think we would encourage a gentleman who did not?"

Diana stood, weary of their inability to see her point of view. "Then I shall look forward to dancing with him at the ball. But for now, I am quite fatigued and have a monstrous headache. Would you have the kitchen send me up some willow bark tea?"

Her father at least had the heart to nod, although Cordelia looked like she would have liked to have said more. She left them and as she was closing the door, she heard Cordelia say, "It will be a relief when she marries and her exploits are not yours to explain."

Diana's hand stayed on the doorknob. She should not listen, but how could she not?

"I hope Colonel Webster has the marriage license in hand. We should use it at his earliest convenience. I met with Templeton at the stables. He has compromised her somehow on the road, I am sure of it, and is determined to marry her. Nothing I said took the light of hope from his eyes."

Her heart fell. Not just for the confirmation they both wanted to be rid of her, but because the door was closing shut on any other way out. Marriage license and no banns. Immediate marriage. Her breath caught in her throat and refused to budge.

"He only wants her money," Cordelia said. Often a person stated things that were actually their own motivations. Was that why Cordelia had married her father?

"He loves her, too, I have no doubt. But I'll not have her inheritance poured into that place."

That was enough. She didn't need to hear them disparage Templeton's good name while she listened. There was no way Templeton only wanted her money. She knew him well enough to know he would tell Father to keep the dowry if that was the only hurdle.

If only that were the only hurdle.

CHAPTER 20

IN WHICH TREASURE FALLS IN TEMPLETON'S LAP

Malmsbury stood in the center of the stables, surrounded by a ring of sporting types and hussars. He'd made it to Brighton in just over five hours, not quite beating the Prince of Wales's time. But then, in the interests of keeping the prince happy, nobody really wanted to do that.

After taking a detour outside to calm his anger, Alec strolled to the edge of the group. The afternoon sun dropped lower in the sky, bathing the stables and Captain Malmsbury in golden light as he captivated them with his story.

A hussar interrupted him. "But what about the piece by the side of the road I heard about? Did you see her? Williams arrived not ten minutes ago with a wild story."

Malmsbury swung around to him. "The chit by the side of the road crying? I thought to myself *likely story*! I drove past her like the wind, her wails following me into Horley."

Everyone laughed heartily. Then Malmsbury spotted Alec. "Ah, Templeton, did you drive past the damsel in distress, or were you lured in?"

"Well and truly snagged," he replied. "She even tried to shoot me, and that's when I clipped her accomplice, Douglas. I have to go back to the magistrate on my way home." Best to lay the foundation for the story now. It would be all around the room within an hour that Alec had made the shot and not his companion.

The assembled men nodded and murmured their support. "Dashed hard to drive past a lady," one said.

Alec nodded and then leaned across to Malmsbury. "A word, if I might?"

Malmsbury swung around and scanned Templeton's face. "My fellow racer must steal me for a moment, chaps. Will I see you all at The Ship later? Pints are on me." They cheered their agreement, and Malmsbury joined Alec, who led him toward the octagonal-shaped horse-drinking station that looked more like a fountain in the middle of the stable.

Alec leaned against the edge. "I would like to ask you some questions about the race, and I hope, as a fellow member of Wrack and Ruin, that you can help me."

Malmsbury bowed. "As a fellow member of Wrack and Ruin, I would do anything for you."

Templeton looked at him steadily, and Malmsbury's gaze darted away. "I am glad to hear it. Because if you mean to recoup your lost fortunes, I don't believe that aiding and abetting the people who stole this race is perhaps the way to do it."

Malmsbury paled, and his gaze darted around the room, seeing if anyone was listening to their conversation. He swallowed and met Alec's gaze steadily. "I don't know what you mean, but tread carefully, Lord Templeton, because it sounds like you're accusing me of cheating. Why the bookmakers wouldn't even allow me to place a bet on myself."

Bookmakers, who laid odds on each entrant so that no matter who won they made a profit, normally kept themselves to the racetrack at Newmarket. That they had expanded out to this race was of interest. But not taking a bet from Malmsbury was even more telling. "Unusual. They normally take a wager from anyone on anything at any time."

Bow Street needed to be involved, and he was more than happy to do it. How much did Malmsbury know of their plans?

A plump-in-the-pocket bookmaker would have enough blunt to make certain things happen along the road to Brighton. And theirs was an industry with no laws. If they saw a prize worth taking, they would use whatever means were at their disposal to win it. These were the same people that bribed jockeys to pull on a horse's reins to slow it down, or made sure it was fed something before a race that would slow it down.

"Well, they wouldn't take a wager from me. And, they convinced me not to drink the night before if you can believe it. Dashed if I don't have more of a headache from *not* drinking than I normally do *from* taking ale!" He laughed at his own joke. "But at least I—"

"Stop." Alec cut him off. "This is no laughing matter. Pip could have died from that branch, I could have died from a fully loaded pistol, and multiple entrants were kidnapped. But nothing happened to you. Strange, no?" Alec waited a long moment, drawing out his eye contact with Malmsbury. "So, I accuse you of nothing. Yet. But if there is something to find, rest assured, Beaufort and I will find it."

He would hire runners himself to find the people behind it, so they didn't think they could do this kind of thing again.

The smile disappeared from Malmsbury's face. He rubbed the gold buttons on his waistcoat around and around. "You speak for Beaufort?"

Alec nodded, flexing his hand. "In this instance, I know I can." Viscount Beaufort, their club's founder, would be no more impressed than he.

"Interesting." Malmsbury took a step back and crossed his arms over his chest. "You know, I was on the Steine earlier and I could swear I saw, well, I can't be right, but it looked *very much* like Miss Kingsley alighting from your carriage. In men's garb, no less. Why would that be?"

The hairs on the back of his neck stood up. To think he thought they'd escaped notice. But to Malmsbury he merely rolled his eyes. "That is your response? To attempt blackmail on a young lady who, last time I saw her, was in Sutton?"

He shrugged. "I know what I saw. And while I'm sure there were a great many injustices on the road to Brighton today, I had no hand in them. But I don't need you muddying the waters of my win. If you don't besmirch my name to Beaufort, I won't besmirch Miss Kingsley's name either." He smiled, entirely smug. "Seems like a fair trade? You've known the family for a long time, I believe?"

Alec wanted to push him right into the horses' watering fountain and watch the water drip from his mustache.

"I know that look," Malmsbury said. "You sweet on her? Don't blame you. Dashed fine female."

Alec took a step forward, one step closer to Malmsbury landing where he belonged. They were of similar height, and Alec would have the element of surprise.

He closed his eyes. He was a *gentleman* and a peer of the realm. He did not throw other gentlemen into horse troughs, even if it was tempting. *Oh, so tempting.*

"She might be Lady Luck—but she's not so lucky in love, if you know what I mean." Malmsbury smiled in a leery way that suggested he had superior knowledge of Diana's love life.

That's it.

Malmsbury didn't see the threat and made the mistake of leaning against the trough. He continued on. "Jilts Fortescue at the altar with a *horse* no less, and now ready to be shackled to that bounder Webster. That tells me the family is desperate to fire her off to just about anyone."

Alec took one step forward but stopped when the word

"bounder" reached his consciousness. He frowned. "Why do you call him a bounder?"

Malmsbury shrugged his shoulder. "For that is my personal experience. You see, he was my commanding officer, before I joined the hussars. The eighty-ninth Regiment of Foot in Malta. I was surprised to hear Miss Kingsley was betrothed to him, because I am certain that he has a Maltese lady with whom he has a son. We were there over two years for that siege. She is a very religious lady and would not be unmarried. It may have been a papist marriage, but it was a marriage nonetheless."

With whom he has a son? Oh. Alec's world shifted from under him, and the round stables seemed to spin. Webster was about to commit bigamy? So much for him being a paragon. He was a scoundrel of the first order!

And *this* was a scandal of proportions bigger than Fortescue. This was the kind of scandal that could break Diana and her family, if not handled gently.

Captain Malmsbury boxed his hands in front of him. "There now. I have made you a gift of information that would surely be a bigger scandal for her than wearing a greatcoat. We're even, yes?"

Alec shook his head in disbelief. "We're even? So, I'm supposed to look the other way while you make off with thousands of guineas in prize money, because you tell me something any normal gentleman would think was a matter of honesty and honor?"

He held Alec with a steady gaze. "Yes. I swear I had nothing to do with any of the happenings on the road today."

Alec crossed his arms across his chest, mostly to stop himself from taking the final step and pushing him in. "I think not. Unless you do me a small favor."

A quiet word with Webster should surely be enough to make him cry off? And if he could keep himself out of the entire thing, all the better. After all, last time all he'd done was make sure she could overhear a conversation that would tell her how her future husband truly saw their marriage and next thing he knew, there was a horse walking down the aisle.

But surely a connection of the Duke of Wellsmore would not want his papist marriage bandied about society, and would quietly exit the scene, leaving Diana free to marry him.

Surely.

He didn't grow up surrounded by peers of the realm, who would go to any lengths to protect their reputation, to misread this situation.

Webster would retreat like an army man faced by a hoard of enemy forces.

For the first time, a future with Diana was within his grasp. He just had to tread gently. But he could be as soft as the down on a duckling when the situation required.

"What's the small favor?" Malmsbury was looking wary.

"A tiny thing. But you must be subtle and seek out Webster quietly. I would have him discreetly break off his engagement to Miss Kingsley."

Malmsbury's eyes flared. "No. I cannot. It would mean never getting another promotion. Too much to ask of a man. And over a silly chit, too." He shook his head and stood straighter. "Won't do it."

"Of course you won't. Heaven forbid you should do something to help someone other than yourself. I'm not sure you understand the base requirement of being in Wrack and Ruin is the willingness to help others."

Alec leaned forward, put both hands on Malmsbury's chest and shoved him backward into the trough before he could register what was happening. "Let's see if a little cold water brings you some sense."

He went in bottom first, arms flailing and trying to grab the stone edge as he fell. But it was no use. Even if his legs were still hanging over the edge, his entire top half was in the water. "Damn it, you'll pay for this. You've ruined my coat."

"Not your boots, though," Alec said, pinching his toe. "Hoby *will* be glad to see they've come through today unscathed. See you at the next Wrack and Ruin meeting. It should be a good one."

He sauntered away, leaving someone else to haul Malmsbury out.

At least something went right today, and it felt far better than it should have.

CHAPTER 21

WHERE SLEEPING IN THE ATTIC HAS DECIDED BENEFITS

The next morning, close to dawn, when the sun's rays were only a soft glow on the horizon, Diana heard the unmistakable sound of something on the roof above her.

Uncle Horatio's townhouse was not the largest in Brighton and she had been relegated to a room directly under the roof, with such a low-pitched ceiling that it felt more like a ship's cabin. She stilled and eyed the roof hatch, a square opening in the middle of the ceiling, with trepidation.

The hatch quietly slid away. Heart racing, she jumped from the bed to the fireplace to pick up a poker.

"It's me," a hushed voice said through the open crack.

"Alec?" Her heart continued to race.

"Who else? Daniel told me you were in the attic room. He put a convenient ladder on the side of the building, so I took a chance and hoped for the best."

Who else? It could be thieves coming to rob the house, and there she was standing in her nightgown. But it was Alec and, despite knowing that nothing was going to change the situation, everything felt lighter just to see him.

His hand appeared. "Here, catch." Something dropped from the hole, and her reflexes reached for it before she even knew what it was. She stared down at a small posy of pink rosebuds, their stems wrapped in a white ribbon. "How sweet."

He pulled the hatch open a little further. "But slightly thorny."

"Like me." She smiled up at him.

He smiled in response. "I may also have discovered something to help us in our cause, but it's too early to tell."

It piqued her interest, but also a fair dose of alarm. "Don't do anything until you are sure. We must be sure."

"I agree. A quick question. Do you know anything about Colonel Webster's past? For example, is he a widower?"

She paused, thinking of all the conversations they had about his life. "He does not like to talk about war time. I know more about where he grew up, and Eton, than I do about his adult life." It was almost as if he had gone from being a studious schoolboy who read law at Cambridge, to the gentleman who was about to embark on a glittering diplomatic career.

Alec frowned. "It is understandable not to want to speak of war time. But if you know nothing more, I shall have to find it out myself."

She pulled on his hand. "Do be careful. He is one of England's heroes and we don't want to embarrass him."

"Oh yes, very heroic," he said in a bitter and sarcastic tone. *What had he discovered?*

"Come down and tell me what you know." She would dearly like to be held in his arms, although that was probably a very bad idea.

"I can't. No way to get back up. Unless you have a handy ladder in your room?"

"No, I don't." She shook her head and crossed the room to pick up the chair by the small desk and perch it under the hatch. Then she climbed up. The attic room had a low ceiling, and she was now close enough to touch him.

"I like your nightgown," he whispered.

It was a monstrosity that enveloped her from neck to toe, so she wasn't sure what he meant. Instead of asking, she reached up to touch his hand. "Thank you."

"For the nightgown compliment, or for the flowers?" He gripped her hand, then threaded his fingers through hers. To touch him without gloves felt electric. To do it standing in her nightgown was incendiary.

"For coming to see me."

He squeezed her hand. "I am working on our problem."

"I don't envisage you having much luck. Father and Cordelia mean to make me do my duty. *I* mean to make me do my duty. How can I do anything else when to cry off would create the very scandal I'm trying to avoid?"

He nodded. "I understand, and I resent Webster's entire being."

Diana shook her head. "The blame does not rest with Colonel Webster. I accepted his offer of marriage with no compulsion. If I have had the offer of my dreams in the meantime, that is nobody's fault but my own. I am to visit the Brighton pleasure gardens with him today. I will try to resolve this myself. No scandal involved."

"Ever my intrepid one." Alec moved himself a little, wiggling. "And if you can't, I will. Between us both, we will prevail and without any of the scandal you so wish to avoid."

He sounded very sure of himself, and for the first time since speaking to Father and Cordelia, she allowed herself to hope. She might yet spend her life teasing and goading him.

He looked at her, mischief in his eyes. "Can you move that chair a foot to the left and then get up again?" His head disappeared.

She quietly stepped down, moved the chair and got back up again. What was he up to?

The next moment, he bent waist down from the ceiling so

that if she stood on the balls of her feet, she could … kiss him. She reached up to cup his upside-down face. "Oh my," she said, taking a deep breath.

"It appears I am at your mercy," he said, a cheeky grin belying his words. "As I have always been."

She traced a finger around his jaw. He had not yet shaved and there was a delicious stubble on his normally clean-shaven jaw. She lay a tiny kiss on the corner of his mouth and was rewarded with him stifling a groan. "Totally at my mercy," she whispered.

"Diana." He said her name like a whispered prayer and one only she could answer. And while she would love to tease him, perhaps time was not on her side and she should take full advantage of this delightful situation.

"Oh, very well," she said with a laugh, and kissed him, very slowly, like she had all the time in the world.

It was only later, when he had gone and her lips had stopped tingling and her heart had stopped racing, that she realized he never had told her what he discovered.

CHAPTER 22

IN WHICH COLONEL WEBSTER IS STEADFAST IN ALL THE WRONG WAYS

Later that morning, Diana was escorted by Colonel Webster to the Brighton pleasure gardens with a parasol in her hand and turmoil in her mind. How could she make a break with him that would not impinge on her honor, or his?

He didn't deserve any scandal being attached to his name. That was all she knew. Unlike Fortescue, he had done nothing wrong and still had her respect. Aside from his questionable treatment of horses, that was.

The problem was that she didn't know him well enough to know what would outrage him enough to jilt her. The only certainty was that he wanted her to be a model of decorum, so she would just have to proceed along those lines.

Cordelia was overly courteous to the colonel when he arrived, perhaps hoping to remind Diana of where her duty lay. As though she could forget. Even the gardens were at odds with her, the late summer bloom of the geraniums a jubilant display in oranges and pinks the opposite of her mood.

It was a good thing there were so many flowers to distract her, because Diana could scarcely look at Colonel Webster's face.

How could she marry this man she barely knew? Or would his gentlemanly manners extend to releasing her when he realized they would not suit?

Cordelia would tell her that an engaged heart was not a requirement of marriage, and perhaps she was right. But knowing Alec loved her made that feel more wrong than ever.

The colonel was dressed beautifully today, taking great pains with a cravat that looked like a linen waterfall. His chocolate-colored superfine molded his shoulders and his boots shone to perfection. His valet had done him proud. Worse than that, he was making interesting and polite conversation. Diana paid closer attention.

"And then the prince said the tradesmen were all ungrateful and should be happy for the employment! I ask you, how is gratefulness going to feed their families? That man runs up debt like it's a pastime."

He now had her complete attention, considering that Alec was in a similar position of being owed money by the prince. "But he will pay them, surely? I imagine he has used every skilled trade in the region to build those stables. He would hurt the entire town."

Webster shrugged. "It remains to be seen. But I have heard many stories of his personal debts going on for many years and him considering the money *gifts*. It literally takes an act of parliament for his debts to be paid, because they are so far beyond his allowance."

So, Alec would need an act of parliament to get his fortune back? That sounded near impossible. Her heart wrung at the thought.

"Don't worry your head about those tradesmen. I'm sure they will get paid, eventually."

Colonel Webster was pleasant and affable, and Diana couldn't help hoping he would not be too offended when she outlined how she was not the pinnacle of ladyhood he deserved. Because it was the only way out.

"I must tell you what I did on the way here to Brighton." Her voice held an unbidden tremor.

He raised his eyebrows, inviting her to continue her story. "Tell me, what could a lady possibly get up to on the brief trip down to Brighton?"

"Well, my friend Beth and I stayed at The Cock in Sutton, which was the end of the first stage of the race, hoping to support Pip as he drove through." It was as good a place as any to start.

"Yes, your father told me that. He asked my approval, if you must know, although I have no idea why. I cannot stop you doing anything while you are still under his roof! But I did appreciate his forethought."

Diana glossed over the fact that her father had seen it necessary to inform her fiancé of her movements. Or that after their marriage, Webster considered it within his power to stop her from doing anything. She shook the thoughts away. They weren't important at the moment. "In any case, Pip came into the change injured and could no longer ride."

He stopped walking, his eyes wide. "Goodness, I hope he wasn't badly hurt. How ever did he keep going?"

"Oh, he didn't," said Diana blithely. "*I* did." She stopped walking, and he took a couple of steps onward as he digested what she just said. *Please be outraged. Please realize I am not good enough to be the wife of a diplomat on His Majesty's Service.*

He turned to her in astonishment. "Are you telling me *you* drove in the race and crossed the finish line yesterday and *not* your brother?"

So far, so good. "Templeton drove across the finish line. He dropped me off with my valise just beforehand on the Steine. Father said I should hope you never find out," Diana stared down at her hands. "However, I am an honest creature and believe in transparency, especially with the man I am to wed. I had no plans to compete in the race, but when my brother was not able to, I found myself in that curricle and riding down the Brighton Road before I really understood the consequences of my actions. It is often thus with me. I was also alone with Templeton for the last quarter of the race." She tilted her head to one side. "I'm sure that's not good either."

She took a few more steps, trying to read his expression. It was as calm and expressionless as always, although there was a pulse in his jaw that suggested he was not entirely unmoved by her admission.

Finally, he looked up at her and smiled almost ruefully, taking her hand. "You were in an open carriage, so no harm done with Templeton. I won't tell anyone if you don't. I suppose it is to be expected that as indulged and cosseted as an only daughter can be, your behavior leaves something to be desired. I appreciate your honesty, for I feel that at the very least it shows a willingness to change. We shall rub along well together. Your father is obviously indulgent, but that does not make for a harmonious house. You know what is required of you and where your duty lies, as a wife and, one day, as a mother."

Her breath seemed caught in her chest. This conversation was *not* going as planned. He was supposed to fly into the boughs, realize she was not wifely material, and offer to quietly dissolve their engagement. Proving once again that she did not know Colonel Webster at all. He had more steel in him than his benign exterior suggested.

It also looked like there was no escaping it. *One last try.* "I fear I am unlikely to change. I love horses, and I love driving, and I will continue to do so when we are wed."

If she was hoping for him to say something like "I think not," she was sorely disappointed. Instead, he shrugged, like that was of no concern to him. "Of course you will. I'm sure you will. Although many of the pursuits you enjoyed in childhood will fall away under the rigors of running a household.

And you may not find yourself wanting to ride in the Calcutta heat. I know I certainly just want to sit in the shade most of the time."

"Oh." She hadn't thought of that.

He pulled her arm through his as they continued around the garden. "I think I understand what's going on here. Your sudden honesty and admission to your faults, point to only one thing. Bridal nerves." He smiled at her, smug. "I understand. But you have nothing to fear in me. You'll find me a most reasonable husband and master. Indeed, I have settled on a lovely house in Calcutta. I knew the moment I saw the painting that you would love it. Do not think for a moment that your exuberance is off-putting to me. Not in the least. I could never marry a lady without spirit. Now let's not talk about this any longer. Let's enjoy our walk."

There seemed little more she could say. She would not embarrass him by letting him know she loved another man. What was the point? "Very well. But if I am not the right lady for you, I'm sure we can come to some sort of amicable solution. I do not want to be married to a man who does not esteem me *as I am.*" She could not even bring herself to say the word *love,* because that had never been part of their bargain.

He turned to her with a mischievous light in his eye. "Oh I respect you *greatly!* Never fear, you will not be sending the horse down the aisle for me, my girl, so get that thought out of your head."

He had no intention of politely freeing her from the engagement.

"Indeed. He is not mine to send any longer. You are quite safe."

Damn his eyes.

Then she remembered what Templeton had asked her in the soft dawn light. "Colonel Webster?"

He took a deep breath. "Clive, remember?"

She nodded. "Of course. I was wondering, are you a widower? I never thought to ask."

His body tensed, but he covered quickly and patted her hand. "We have our whole lives to discover all the little things about each other. But, no, I am not a widower. Not that it would matter if I were, I'm sure."

"No. Of course not." She poked the grass with her suede boot.

"Stop worrying. Let me take care of everything," Colonel Webster said. "I think I am now in agreement with Cordelia. We should use the marriage license sooner rather than later and settle matters between us. I can see that given too much time to think, you have anxious tendencies. Let's set a date. How does next Thursday sound? A small wedding. Just our immediate family. What say you?"

He was waiting for an answer, but the sadness that overcame Diana stole her words away.

"There now, I have shocked you. All will be well." He picked up her hand and brought it to his lips.

She nodded, willing the tears that gathered in her eyes to go away. They would not, and as she bent looking at the grass, one dropped onto the blue suede of her boot, creating a dark blue circle.

Fight, Diana, damn you.

But she had fought. With every weapon she had. She'd just lost, that was all.

CHAPTER 23

IN WHICH OPERA IS JUST THE BACKDROP FOR DRAMA

The festivities were to begin at four, with the announcement of the race winner, followed by a sunset concert on the Promenade Grove by famous opera singer Sarah Hayworth, then the ball.

Stephen had the nous to take the curricle to The Old Ship where Alec had a room, and so he luckily had all his evening attire for the stay in Brighton. It would have been very awkward if Stephen had returned to London with his bag.

Had he chosen the hotel on the same street as Uncle Horatio to be close to Diana? Why, of course, he had. Although he hadn't realized she would be driving in the race when he'd sent the letter to bespeak the room.

Dressed in his evening finery, Alec walked up Ship Street in time to see the Kingsleys enter their carriage for the event. As Mrs. Kingsley stepped up, by some sixth sense, Diana turned, stilling as she saw him, her eyes wide. She had eschewed the usual white muslin evening gown for one of royal blue, her golden hair artfully swept up and adorned with a single white feather on her headpiece.

He stopped breathing for a moment. She was so beautiful.

That she might soon be the wife of another man, if he didn't do something, was like a spike to his heart.

She threw him a soft smile, lifting her hand and letting it drop again. Then she stepped into the carriage. Mr. Kingsley unfortunately followed his daughter's gaze and spotted Alec, too. He lifted his walking cane, unsmiling, and followed them in.

Three in the carriage, but no offer to take him up with them. *Ah, well.* It wasn't as if Mr. Kingsley was wrong. Alec *was* planning to ruin Diana's engagement.

Again.

So he walked. It was a beautiful evening for it, and Brighton was made for promenading. He arrived at the gardens before the Kingsleys, as the carriages were put in a cue to drop their passengers at the gates to the marine pavilion. So, he wandered through to the small stage that had been erected in front of the stables.

Alec took a glass of champagne from a server and stood under a tree to wait until he saw someone he knew. He did not join Diana's group when they arrived, for Colonel Webster was there and Alec's dissembling skills weren't good enough to hide his disgust of a man who would commit bigamy to marry an heiress. And this was not the right place for that particular confrontation. For that, he needed proof and privacy.

His promise to keep everything discreet would be kept.

He was just wondering if he had arrived too early, when he spotted the prince's aide, Major Bloomfield, flitting from group to group like a regimental butterfly.

All the letters he had previously sent to the prince's office had been returned with a polite note signed by Major Bloomfield. They may have never been introduced, but they certainly knew each other. He searched the crowd for someone to introduce them, landing on Mr. Vulliamy who would undoubtedly be acquainted with the major. And was also acquainted with Alec, since he had made sure all debts to the talented clockmaker had been paid in full. This was too good an opportunity to pass up. It would be worth the hundred-guinea entry fee just for an inter-view with him.

Within a few minutes, Mr. Vulliamy was leading him to the major and had made the introductions. Major Bloomfield looked less than pleased and shot the master craftsman a glare.

Alec looked around in amusement. "I see a want of money does not interfere with the entertainment this evening."

The major blinked, unamused. "I know what you want, Lord Templeton, and I can't help you."

Alec closed his eyes briefly. "I have been very patient, and perhaps I could continue to be so, if my own predicament were not so dire."

"It is hardly the prince's fault that your father was so generous with him. A wonderful friend. Now if you will excuse me?"

So, he was to receive the same polite rebuff in person. There was no debt, just very generous gifts. He might have believed that before he'd put in the hours of searching and research. "Be prepared to explain your refusals when you are answering to the cabinet, Major Bloomfield. I am *not* going away. This is not just about me, but the people on my land and their future. You force me to take steps I would rather not take. Very public steps. Unless you consider an initial payment."

The major straightened, and his gaze narrowed. "And what would that be?"

Alec went for broke. No point running a race if you stalled before a fence. "I will not make these claims public if the first payment is in the form of a horse. Equinox, to be exact."

The major laughed. "I shall tell the prince you want his prize stallion. Best of luck to you." He shook his head. "But I doubt you can even prove the debt. Many before you have failed."

It was time to play his trump card, although letting the major know might endanger his case. "I have a stack of signed IOUs that suggest otherwise."

The major's eyes widened and then narrowed in suspicion. "Do you? I wager they are forged."

Alec looked off into the distance as if the entire conversation had become tiresome, although the opposite was true. "They are not. It just took me some time to find and gather them. Shall I hear from you soon, then?"

Bloomfield bowed. "No, you will not. Get yourself another glass of champagne and enjoy your evening. If I see you try to approach the prince, I will have his guard escort you out."

Typical army man to have such an inscrutable face and stiff rump. Frustration bubbled inside him, like a keg of gunpowder about to ignite.

Vulliamy turned to him. "That was predictable. He owes my establishment a small fortune, and yet continues to order watches and clocks from us at an astonishing rate."

"That does not breed hope," Alec answered. It seemed the prince never learned from his lessons and just continued to gather debt with joyful abandon.

They both watched in silence as the marshal made his way up to the stage and called to gather the crowd. They were already mostly walking toward the stage, having been ushered there by staff.

Alec looked in the crowd for Diana, seeing her at the edge with Colonel Webster and no guardians in sight. He supposed as an engaged lady they gave her more license with Webster.

Just looking at the man made Alec feel ill. But Diana was right. He had to confirm the facts of the case before he took any steps to approach either Webster or Mr. Kingsley. He would have to keep his distance tonight, because he didn't trust himself not to plant Webster a facer. England's hero or not.

The marshal brought his attention back to the stage. "Welcome, ladies and gentlemen and of course our distinguished guests. The Prince of Wales welcomes you to his new stables! Isn't it a sight to behold?"

The assembled crowd politely applauded.

"Unfortunately, our race, sponsored by the prince, has not been so splendid. Many of you may have heard of the mischief on the road yesterday, everything from kidnappings, to tack being cut, to shots being fired. I do not need to tell you that none of this is in the spirit of fair play." He held up his hand when the crowd started chattering among themselves like they were at the opera. "And we have called for Bow Street to be involved in bringing those responsible to justice."

Alec started in surprise. That was unexpected good news. He would make sure he spoke to the marshal about his suspicions of the Newmarket bookmakers. And Malmsbury.

"What this means, is that we, the race committee, feel that awarding a winner tonight would be imprudent and would only encourage this kind of behavior for any future races that are held."

There were cries of outrage from where Malmsbury and his crew of soldiers were standing. "Unfair!"

"What about our entry fees?"

The marshal focused on the person who had asked the question. "Indeed. All your entry fees will be returned with an extra ten pounds from the prince for the trouble you have gone to. Apologies one and all, but we will not change our mind on this. It was not a fair race, so there cannot be a fair winner."

At least he would get his hundred guineas back.

"But who actually won?" Captain Malmsbury asked.

"We will declare no winner. Indeed, we did not finish calculating it once we heard what had happened. Nobody knows. What I can tell you is that nobody beat the prince's time to Brighton. His record of four-and-a-half hours still stands."

The crowd cheered, and Alec noted that the prince himself was now part of the crowd, standing with his cronies in a happy, and likely drunk, group. He bowed to the marshal.

At least the criminals behind it would not prosper. With no

winner, they could not pay out winnings, and gambler's money would have to be returned. He should feel better about not only getting his entry fee back but making ten pounds extra. He'd also made headway talking to Major Bloomfield and fired the first shot across the bow to the prince about the outstanding debts.

So why did it feel like he'd lost everything?

One look at Diana answered the question. She stood next to her fiancé, head bent and eyes sad. And next to her was Webster, who likely had a papist wife and had no problem at all marrying an innocent woman when he was already married. Where was the justice there?

No, life was never won by the good or the just. It was the scoundrels who took the day.

CHAPTER 24

IN WHICH CORDELIA PROMISES TO EAT HER BONNET

They had lost. Of course they had. At least the criminals had not won, but it still made her heart ache when they toured the stables and found her boy in his stall, when she had been hoping to win enough money to take him home with her.

He was roped off so that nobody could touch him, but he stirred when he heard her voice and the guard let her through. "There, there, you are *such* a good boy," she said soothingly. He snorted in reply, and her other hand was nudged by Honey, who also thought she deserved a pat and some kind words.

"Yes, Honey. You are a splendid girl." She opened her reticule, which she had filled with pitted dates for just this occasion, and fed them to her horses. *No, not her horses anymore.* She blinked away the beginning of a tear.

Colonel Webster waited for her on the other side of the ropes. "Come now, Miss Kingsley. The sooner you leave them, the sooner they can forget you."

She looked up at him, dismayed that tears were welling in her eyes. Again. She hadn't cried in years, and now she'd cried twice in one day. "If you think a horse *ever* forgets *anyone* they love, then ..." She let the sentence hang, but what she wanted to say was, *then you are a greater fool than I thought.* She gave them the last of her dates and whispered in Equinox's ear. "I will be back for you. We will ride together again. But until that day, eat as many of the prince's oats as you can."

Colonel Webster smiled indulgently when she came to him, pulling her arm through his. "There now. Your love of your horses does you credit."

Who cares what does me credit? She nodded demurely, not trusting herself to speak. Because despite what she'd said to Equinox, perhaps she *would* never see him again. If they could find no way out of this engagement that wouldn't hurt everyone around her. If she married and went to Calcutta, this may be the last time she saw her beautiful boy.

They exited the stables to find that dusk had settled, and the colorful lanterns that hung from every low-lying branch had been lit, creating a Vauxhall-like atmosphere to the prince's gardens. It was the grand kind of opening one would expect from the Prince of Wales. Only the very best of everything, champagne in crystal glasses, an orchestra, and famous opera singer La Luminosa's soprano mixing with the sound of blackbirds nesting for the night.

All this to celebrate a place where horses slept. Diana smiled to herself. Templeton would add up what this cost and wonder how the prince could sleep at night.

Colonel Webster searched her face. "What amuses you? Not that I'm complaining to see you smile, finally."

She ignored the slight barb. "Oh, just the thought of all this excitement for some stables."

"You must admit, they are beautiful." He turned toward the gigantic dome where the final rays of sun reflected off the many panels of glass. It gave the garden a lush, overblown feeling, and everyone was euphoric, like the last kick of warmth before they had to brace for the cold.

"Oh, most worthy." But they were still just a place for a horse to sleep and exercise.

Webster bowed as Cordelia and Father approached. They stopped under a grouping of Chinese lanterns. The area had been deserted as the crowd had flocked to watch the concert now in progress.

"Good evening, again," Father said, giving them both an approving smile. It should have felt better to do her duty, but alas, it was like biting into a lemon.

Diana spent the next few moments making an argument in her head that if there was no other way, this good man would be a more than adequate husband, and she would soon put paid to his slightly controlling ways. Once she had children, perhaps she would not be expected to go abroad for his postings. Then her life might then be lived purely on her own terms. She could live in a loveless marriage. Women did it every day.

There, that felt better. She could even look at him and smile.

"Your gown is very becoming," Colonel Webster said. "Did you choose the color, Miss Kingsley? The blue is beautiful on you."

Diana nodded. "You are very kind. My dressmaker, Madam La Favre, chose the color. She always knows what is most suitable." Diana shivered. The weather was not quite perfect. A sea breeze had picked up while they had toured the stables, with the sun all but gone. The air had a distinct chill.

When she looked around at the gathered crowd, she noticed Captain Malmsbury standing aside from his group of friends, his gaze fixed on her. She threw him a haughty look and turned away, giving him the cut direct. *Please go away.* But when did a man like that ever take a lady's feelings into account?

Oh no. Instead of looking away, he made directly for her little group. The color in his cheeks suggested he may have imbibed a little too much champagne.

"Here comes Captain Malmsbury. He was once one of my

men, you know! Very proud." Colonel Webster clapped his congratulations as Malmsbury arrived. "Well done, Captain, well done. I know they didn't award you the prize, but I heard you likely won in any case."

Captain Malmsbury was in a jovial and somewhat intoxicated mood. It was likely to be expected of a soldier when the champagne was free. He greeted them all loudly, and then his eyes rested on Colonel Webster. He saluted. "Colonel."

Diana searched the crowd, looking for Alec, only to find him frowning at Captain Malmsbury and walking directly toward them. His dark hair brushed his shoulders in poetic waves, and his cravat frothed at his throat, the shirt points only emphasizing his strong jaw. His tailcoat was ink dark, and he wore a deep-purple waistcoat embroidered with flowers.

Her heart fluttered a little and nothing could stop her looking at his lips and remembering how he kissed. She *knew* how he kissed now.

"Oh dear," she heard Cordelia say under her breath. "Whatever can he want?"

Alec's jaw was set, his gaze determined. *What are you doing?* "Nothing nefarious, Cordelia. Please calm yourself. It's just Templeton," Diana replied, smoothing her dress and ignoring the twist of nerves his arrival brought.

"Oh, I don't know," Malmsbury said. "He tipped me into a horse trough this afternoon. Not be trusted."

Cordelia gasped. "How shocking. I hope you were unscathed."

"Just a little wet." He pulled on his cuffs.

Before Cordelia could become more outraged, Templeton arrived and bowed to the group, his gaze lingering on Malmsbury. He smiled as though he hadn't a care in the world. Looks certainly were deceiving. "How lovely to see you all together. Such a wonderful night. I vow I am quite floored by La Luminosa. Miss Kingsley, would you care to venture to the seats to listen to her?" He gave Diana a speaking glance.

He didn't include the group in his invitation, and it was patently obvious he wanted Diana alone. However, while that might be what he wanted, there could be nothing worse for her. Colonel Webster would not allow her to stroll off with Alec and neither would Father. Whatever reason he had for luring her away would have to wait.

"I am happy here, at present," she replied, glaring. *I cannot go with you.*

He returned the same glare, imploring her to come with him. When she shrugged ever-so slightly, he gave up. "Very well. Then will you at least promise me a dance later?"

Diana looked to her father, who nodded slightly. "Yes, thank you. I would be honored."

Alec glanced at her father and pressed his lips together briefly before smiling. "The honor is all mine." Then he looked from her father to her. "I will be listening to the aria, should you wish to find me." He gave Diana another speaking glance.

"We'll join you there soon, Templeton," Father said, as close as anyone could get to shooing a peer of the realm away.

A pulse ticked in Alec's clenched jaw, suggesting he was anything but happy, but when Diana nodded, he bowed, and left them.

Malmsbury turned back to the conversation. "Now, Colonel Webster. I've not seen you since Malta. Must be, what, five years ago? How is that lovely wife of yours, and your son, he'd be well out of leading strings now?"

Diana drew in a shocked breath.

Wife?

It couldn't be true. No man would offer marriage when he was already married. If nothing else, Colonel Webster had always struck her as a gentleman of honor.

Shocked silence descended over their party. It didn't seem to affect Malmsbury, who kept on talking as if he hadn't just dropped a grenade on them. "I thought I saw her in Gunter's just a couple of months ago! Never tell me you brought that beautiful Maltese flower into dreary old England?" He laughed. "Although I would be hard pressed to have her away from me for any length of time. Can't blame you!"

"I don't know what you're talking about." Colonel Webster stiffened and his eyes were slits. "You're intoxicated."

"Come, don't play the possum with me. If you didn't want anyone to know about your papist marriage, perhaps you shouldn't have had her host so many parties for us! Best dinners in Malta, upon my honor. No shame in a papist marriage. Be proud of your beautiful wife." He looked around the group. "She is lovely, you know. A dark beauty. Quite the temper!" He waggled his finger at Colonel Webster. "Don't look at me so. You know it's true."

Everyone looked to her. Waiting for her to explode. Just like that fateful cricket match all those years ago, when Fortescue's true character had come to the surface. She took a small step away from them and took a deep breath of salty sea air. She was made of sterner stuff now. She must calm this situation. She put a hand on Malmsbury's arm. "I am sure you are mistaken, Captain Malmsbury. You see, Colonel Webster is betrothed to me."

Captain Malmsbury swallowed hard and suddenly seemed entirely sober. "Yes, I know, my dear. It's a crime. A friend made me realize I have a duty to let you know about it. I hope that when this horrible shock wears off, you will thank me."

A friend? You mean Alec. Her anger surged in a most unladylike way. In fact, her fingers itched to slap him. "I *might* have thanked you if you'd done this privately, rather than at the prince's party."

She was hanging on to the threads of her composure. She turned to her Colonel Webster with a tight smile. If she asked him, she would be able to tell directly if he was lying. "Is this true, Clive?"

What a spectacular first time to use his given name.

The entire party waited for his answer. The soaring sounds of a Mozart aria gave backdrop to the drama playing right in front of her. She pulled her shawl around herself, suddenly cold. If this were true, she would not be marrying him, but the scandal of it would be just as bad as the last time. Just as ruinous to her family.

A dull red flushed up his cheeks, and he looked at Captain Malmsbury as though he'd like to draw a sword on him. "Keep your voice down, please. Of course it's not true. Would I ask Miss Kingsley to marry me if I was not free to marry? Would I put my entire future career at risk? No." He sneered at Malmsbury. "This man, always reckless under my command, drinks too much and has a vivid imagination."

Malmsbury drew himself up straight. "As you wish, Colonel Webster. My apologies for intruding. I think I'll refill my champagne," He backed away. "Good evening to you all."

He left them in a shocked silence, and Diana rounded on Colonel Webster. "Sir?" Their party was far enough away not to draw attention if she was careful. "I believe I asked if you were married, not if you were free to marry. The Prince of Wales himself was free to marry Princess Caroline even though he was married to Mrs. Fitzpatrick. The truth, if you please."

His nostrils flared, and a bead of sweat broke out on his forehead. He wiped it with his handkerchief. "How dare you impugn me?"

Father looked at Cordelia, but she seemed to be able to do nothing but blink. "I think it might be best if you just answer Diana's question. The truth always has a way of coming out in the end. So it behooves you to make a clean breast of this now."

Diana rounded on Colonel Webster again. "Sir?"

Father put his arm around her, lending her his strength. "A simple answer, Webster."

Webster looked far into the distance, as though recalling something from a long time ago. He sighed deeply. "It is true. Although she is not in London. She is still in Malta. We are estranged. Have been for almost a year. And it was a papist marriage, and I have it on good legal authority they don't count here in England. It is like I am not married at all."

"Don't count?" Diana's mind felt like an empty chamber where the thought, *thank goodness I never loved him*, knocked about like a cricket ball.

Was there something wrong with her? The world seemed full of men, ready to use her for their own purposes. She might have used him, too, but she had not done so married.

The noises of the party faded away until all she could hear was the loud beating of her heart.

Father luckily had words when she had none. "If you think you will marry my daughter now, you have oats for brains. And don't talk to me about legalities. If you married your wife knowing you could get out of it, you are a scoundrel, and if you married her and only want to weasel out of it because Diana fell into your lap, then you are an even bigger one."

Colonel Webster turned red in the face. "This is not the place or time for this conversation."

"It is done now, there is no taking it back. And if I hear a whisper of gossip that my daughter has in any way done anything wrong, you'll be hearing from my solicitor." Father turned his back on him.

"What, like driving in the race to Brighton in place of her brother?"

Damnation, why did I tell him that?

Father turned to him, his eyes wide with surprise. "Why, yes, exactly like that. I can assure you, Diana was with us at every stage of the way to Brighton yesterday, and Templeton rode the curricle when Pip was injured. Say what you will. It is our word against that of a bigamist who tried to trick a young innocent lady into marriage."

"You are not good ton, Beau Kingsley," Webster said under his breath. "To say these things in a public place is shameful."

Father clenched his jaw. "No, I am not," he ground out. "I'm a horse breeder, and I do not pretend to be anything other than that. Good evening." With that, Beau Kingsley, the man who thought his entire existence relied on the good opinion of others, turned his back on the nephew of a duke and linked his arm through his daughter's.

Webster strode off, picking a glass of champagne off a passing tray and drinking it in one long gulp.

"Thank you," Diana said. "Although I am scared for what he may do to us."

Father picked up her hand. "I choose you and your needs first." He met her gaze and squeezed her hand. "Somebody wise told me that I should do so more often."

She swallowed the lump in her throat, trying not to cry.

Cordelia had said nothing for the entire scene, and Diana turned to see her regarding the retreating form of Webster with tears in her eyes. "Goodness, Cordelia, pray do not cry. You did not know he was married when you introduced us. I am just glad to have discovered this before we wed."

Cordelia's face twisted in anger. "Oh, you stupid girl. A papist marriage is not a real marriage. Now look at what you have done."

"Cordelia," Father warned, his voice low. "Diana has my full support in this matter."

Cordelia searched Father's face and saw something there that made her swallow and school her features into a ladylike calm. "Very well. I hope you do not live to regret this."

Cordelia might be right. The besmirching of a name so grand as the Websters didn't happen without repercussions.

"I will go and find Templeton," she said blankly.

"Oh, yes," Cordelia replied. "Go and find the man that brought this down on us, for if he didn't know what Captain Malmsbury was about to say, I'll eat my bonnet."

CHAPTER 25

IN WHICH TEMPLETON SHOULD HAVE
KNOWN NOTHING EVER GOES TO PLAN

Diana walked steadily through the crowd, tears streaming down her cheeks, ignoring the stares and the whispers that followed her, letting the angelic voice of the opera singer guide her to Alec. She reached the clearing where seats were placed in a semicircle for the concert. But Alec was not sitting. He was standing at the back, facing her way. He was searching for her, but his face was a carefully constructed mask of boredom.

She knew better.

He spotted her. His eyes flared, and he followed her down the path she took. Any path, as long as it led away from the crowds. He reached for her hands. "What happened?"

The trees made a canopy over the path, and the birds settling down for the night calmed her when her blood wanted to continue roaring. It was disconcerting to have a crisis in such a beautiful place. "Malmsbury told us that Webster has a wife and son in Malta."

Templeton's eyes turned to dangerous slits. "Imbecile."

"Who? Webster or Malmsbury?"

"Both," he said with relish. "There, right there in front of the cream of London society, he lets loose. I suppose he couldn't resist the opportunity to be the center of attention again."

Her heart crashed to the soles of her feet, and folded her arms across her chest. "So you did know?" She whispered it and he heard her because his eyes flashed.

"It was the way I was going to release you from your obligation. But not like this." He closed his eyes. "I asked him to take Webster aside quietly at another time."

The aria rose higher and higher, making her dizzy and confused. Who was right? Who had done the wrong thing? It felt like everyone. She paced a short distance from him and back again. "Why? Why would you take action on such an important decision without consulting me? Help me understand why you took matters into your own hands like it was your right to do so. It might not be your fault that Webster did this now, but it is entirely your fault I was not prepared for it. No warning."

He did not look contrite. Mulish was closer to the mark. "Last time I gave you warning, you sent a horse down the aisle."

She must have heard him wrong. "What do you mean 'last time I gave you warning'?"

He reared back, as though realizing he'd said too much. Eventually he exhaled. "Fortescue. I was the reason you found out he was fortune-hunting. I made sure the information came to you."

And he'd never told her that, although Beth had guessed. "I see. So you have made it quite the habit of interfering in my betrothals without my opinion then." The birds in the bowers above them continued with their night song in contrast to the pounding in her head.

He said nothing, staring resolutely ahead, his mouth a tight, flat line. "I asked Malmsbury to have a quiet word with Colonel Webster so he would just go away. He did not listen."

"Neither did you. I expected more. You are the only person in my world who treats me as though I am intelligent—"

"You *are* intelligent." He ground the words out like she was being obstinate.

"And have the ability to steer my own ship. But when you do something like this …" She lifted both hands in astonishment. "You prove you think I am just as inept as everyone else does. I deserve better." She skewered him with a glare. "I deserve the friend I thought you were."

He reeled back as though she had struck him. "That is truly what you think?"

"You know how strongly I feel about making my own decisions. You cannot say you love me if you take that away from me." And while she had somewhat kept her composure when faced with Webster's duplicity, these words made a lump in her chest that felt like a hot coal radiating out. She hiccuped, then hid her face as the people closed in on them. Her face was flaming.

There was a quiet part of her mind that said 'it's not Alec you are angry at, please stop'. But she didn't listen.

He gripped her hands. "Please don't do this. Give yourself some time to digest what has happened this evening, I beg you."

She twisted away from him. "Now there will be a scandal. I might as well have sent the horse down the aisle again. Everything I did not want to happen, has happened, and I can't control any of it."

He loosened his cravat. "Better that than you just sacrificing yourself on the altar of Kingsley horse sales."

"If it was a sacrifice, it was for the future happiness of the people I love, not horse sales. I cannot have happiness if I am making them wretched in my choices."

"I acted as I did and I don't regret it." His set jaw, normally a source of wonder for her, looked stubborn.

The music stopped, and the air was still. Even the birds had stopped their chirping. She swelled with indignation. "The arrogance of that statement is breathtaking. Not even an *apology* from you." She held up a hand because she couldn't take a moment more. "Enough. Please do me the honor of *not* paying me calls when we return to London."

She turned and walked away, definitely not looking back.

CHAPTER 26

IN WHICH BEAU KINGSLEY'S TIMING WOULD BE HILARIOUS IF IT WEREN'T SO HEARTBREAKING

A few days later, Alec was back in London where the truth about the race, or *The Great Fiasco*, as the newspapers called it, had come out. Bow Street had tracked down the bookmakers involved with the various traps along the road with the help of Douglas and his actress lady. Malmsbury had been interviewed by the newspapers and Bow Street and sheepishly told them everything about his part with the bookmakers. He came off looking like the simpleton he was, but as Alec thought, he had not realized the extent to which the bookmakers were going to influence the race results.

The Prince of Wales announced he had never endorsed the race to start with.

Diana's words still hurt when he thought about them. Which was every other minute. The heat of the moment meant she'd directed all her anger at him, but that didn't mean she was wrong. He'd had a perfectly good chance to tell her what was happening when he'd paid her that morning visit. He'd had plenty of time to tell her about Fortescue in the weeks leading up to the wedding. Both times he'd acted in a way that took away her ability to make a rational decision.

If he was honest, it was because he didn't want her to be rational about these men if it meant she might go through with the marriage to them. There. He'd admitted it. He didn't trust her to make the right decision. *Himself.* She was right.

He was walking toward Brooks, late in the afternoon, when someone drew alongside him, matching his steps. He turned and Beau Kingsley held out his hand. "Well met, friend. You're a hard man to track down," he said. "I have been trying to find you since we arrived back in London."

Friend, was it? Last time he looked, he was *persona non grata* to the Kingsley family. It probably wouldn't be a good idea to let Mr. Kingsley know he was meeting Pip at Brooks. "Ah, yes, well I have been deep in talks with my solicitor to petition the government to repay the prince's debts."

"A good man?"

Considering his good friend Viscount Beaufort had connected them, Alec's trust was implicit. "The very best. He is already working on securing my first payment." But not even correspondence from the office of the Prince of Wales acknowledging the debt could lighten his mood.

If he had lost Diana, he had lost everything. He had penned a letter to her, which he had hoped to give to Pip, but even after five drafts, it wasn't good enough, so he screwed it up and threw it in the fire. He had made decisions without informing her and had withheld information she needed. He deserved her ire.

"If you need anyone to stand with you, or bear witness to the impact giving the prince money had on your estate, I offer my services. We live too close not to have seen and heard the things that went on."

Alec stopped in his tracks, turning to Beau. "My thanks. I believe it is in hand, but if the situation arises, I will contact you."

They walked along St. James Street and into Brooks where the attendants took their coats. "Please don't hesitate. I have been wrong about many things and this might be a way I can make it right. Major Bloomfield was the man who purchased Equinox on behalf of the prince. I may be of use with that connection."

They entered the drawing room and settled at a round table by the window. Pip had not yet arrived. Mr. Kingsley bespoke two glasses of brandy.

His mouth was pressed shut, as though he couldn't quite find the right words.

Interesting.

Alec sat back, ready to be entertained, for Beau Kingsley did not often find himself short of words. "And that leads me to the reason I sought you out."

The brandy arrived, and he took a gulp, as though fortifying himself. "I'm sorry, Alec. I'm sorry for all the times I forbade you courting Diana. I'm sorry for what I said in Brighton. For none of it is true. You are not like your father, and anything you and Diana decided to do with her dowry would be in the best interests of the people at Althorne. I know that."

Anything they decided to do?

Alec nodded and picked up his glass, swirling the brandy before taking a sip. "Thank you." The liquor burned his throat much like this apology.

"And in light of that, I withdraw my opposition and encourage you to court Diana and hope you can marry quite quickly." The last words were said in a rush and he sat back in his chair and exhaled.

"Marry?" Was the man insane? Or once again completely out of touch with his daughter's wishes?

"Well, yes. I suggest that the best way to go about this would be to marry with expediency. Before anyone even realizes she has broken with Colonel Webster. After all, he is the one with more to lose here. He is the one who is currently married and has a wife and son living in Malta."

"Ah." Truth be told, he would take being the best of a bad bunch if it meant he could spend his life with Diana. *But.* "Your permission is quite ironic given that it comes three days on the heels of Diana telling me she never wants to see me again." He laughed. Because if he didn't laugh, he'd likely cry in the drawing room of Brooks. That would be a fun *on-dit* to be spread far and wide.

Mr. Kingsley had the grace to look chagrined. "She was angry, to be sure. But you know her anger dies out fast. You've sparred with her long enough to know that. Under it all, she loves you, Templeton. She has been woeful. Her eyes are red-rimmed eyes and she's taking far too many bruising rides. Cordelia keeps threatening to send her to her aunt in Yorkshire, and I almost agree with her."

He prayed she only suffered because they'd had a falling out and not because she'd decided she would never accept him. "So, she doesn't think of me like a brother, then?"

Mr. Kingsley looked up, his gaze just over Alec's shoulder. "Ah, Pip. Take a seat with us."

Pip organized his coattails and sat, looking from his father to Alec. He was not a lot like his father; where Beau was rake thin and tall, Pip was of average height and muscled. But they both had the same steady gray eyes. "She never thought of you as a brother. Idiotic thought. What are we drinking? Brandy?"

"Are you sure that's wise?" Mr. Kingsley asked. "With your concussion?"

Pip ordered his drink and sat back to wait for it to arrive. "Hard head, as you well know. Right as a trivet now." He looked from Alec to his father. "If we're talking about love, I think I might court Beth. And I'm not asking your permission, although I will ask the vicar, since she's his daughter. Best female of my acquaintance."

"You don't need my approval, but I approve nonetheless," Mr. Kingsley said. "She'll make you a fine wife."

Alec clapped him on the back. "Capital plan. Congratulations.

When she is your wife, can you convince her that I am not the devil incarnate?"

Pip laughed. "Diana can do that when she's *your* wife. Then we'll be brothers, did you think of that?"

"We've been brothers for a while, idiot," Alec replied, affectionately. "But I was just explaining to your father that it is unlikely to happen unless she starts talking to me again."

"Pish posh, Temple. Take action, take control." Pip pumped his fist, and his brandy jumped over the glass and splashed his breeches.

"Of your sister? She has made it quite clear she likes to be in control of her own destiny, and rightly so." He thought about it for a moment. "But I'm not above using everything in my arsenal to convince her. If the past days have shown me anything it's that sometimes fighting dirty wins the day."

He turned to Mr. Kingsley. "Firstly, I want your word that you will find out if this is truly what she wants and honor her decision."

Mr. Kingsley nodded. "Agreed. I have learned my lesson there, too."

"Then, if she says yes, can you have her back in Newmarket this Saturday? Take her on a picnic in the afternoon at say, two?"

Mr. Kingsley nodded. "I can. What should I do, take her to the field near the archery range and just leave her there?"

Pip laughed. "Alec will end up with an arrow lodged in his behind."

"I think not," Alec replied. "If all goes according to plan, perhaps she'll have a change of heart."

"I'll make sure I pack some champagne then," Mr. Kingsley said.

CHAPTER 27

ANYONE FOR A PICNIC?

The autumn leaves rustled outside the stable as Diana groomed Whinny.

Braiding her glossy mane was a good way to cover what she was really thinking about.

Alec.

Kissing Alec.

Wondering if he was ever going to come back. Or if she'd scared him off one too many times with her temper. Had she been a fool, unleashing on him as she had? But he had crossed an important line, and it did her no favors if he thought that was acceptable. But would he come back? Or would she have to go to him?

She reached into her pocket and fished out an apple she had picked from their orchard that morning, and held it in her hand for Whinny to gobble up. "There, see? You let me braid your hair and then you get an apple."

Her father entered the stalls, followed by a maid carrying a picnic basket and a rolled-up blanket. The grooms, who had been warming their bottoms at the fireplace in the tack room, fled to the jobs they likely should have been doing.

Things had been much better between herself and her father, ironically, since the Brighton debacle. It seemed he appreciated the fact she had been willing to do her duty by them, and felt pity for her that once again an engagement had dissolved. This time through no fault of her own.

"There you are. I should have known," Father said. "Would you like to come with me on a picnic?"

Look how hard he was trying. A picnic, for heaven's sake.

"I hear Templeton is back in Newmarket," he said softly. "I also heard that the prince is at least answering his letters now. He might yet get back some of that money he is owed."

Diana stilled her hand on Whinny's mane. "How lovely for him."

"Can I …" He paused, as though weighing his words carefully. "Can I ask if you hold him in your heart?"

Diana nodded, unable to meet his gaze. She pulled a yellow ribbon from her pocket and secured the braid.

"Then I should also tell you, that you have *always* been in his heart, too." He sighed heavily. "I made a mistake that I freely admit. Back when you were seventeen, he asked my permission to court you. I refused. Then a few years ago, after Fortescue, he asked again and I refused. I just thought you would like to know that his admiration for you has been steadfast and not wavered in all these years."

Diana nodded. "He told me. What I don't understand is why you would refuse a man who has always made me happy."

"The debt, of course. And I was waiting to see if he'd turn out like his father. But of course he never did." He shook his head. "Then, in Brighton, he felt so strongly about not being seen as a gold digger that he asked me to cut you off without a penny, and I believe he would have been happy with the results."

"I can imagine him doing that." Probably without asking her if she agreed with his decision. Which she would not, by jove, for that money would be life-changing.

"I could never sentence you to a life of struggle. Oh, I know he has the earldom, but it might as well be a paper crown. I couldn't allow it."

Diana felt tears spring to her eyes. It was most inconvenient, but they refused to stop and ran down her face with abandon. "And now?" she said softly, almost too scared to ask.

"Now I see that he needs you, and that you very much need him, too. You have my blessing. And my apologies. I should have looked at the character of the man and not his current circumstances. I am a fool." He kicked some hay around the stall, then reached up and patted Whinny. "Has he contacted you since Brighton?"

"No." She had at least expected a groveling letter. But nothing. At least not yet. If only she hadn't told Alec never to come around. Now she was going to have to crawl over to Althorne House. Could a lady ask a man to marry her?

"Ah, well. I'm sure he'll come around soon, now that he's back." He motioned to the basket. "But, picnic? Yay or nay? It's chilly, but cook has given us pies fresh from the oven and some cheese."

She leaned forward and kissed him on the cheek. "Thank you, Papa. That sounds lovely."

He offered her his arm, and together they walked from the stables across to the slight hill that was a favorite picnic spot. Large oak leaves crunched under her feet, and the smell of the burning wood from the fireplaces lingered in the air. The trees of the Kingsley estate were turning every shade of orange, red, and yellow, creating their own masterpiece. "You are right, it is a beautiful day for a picnic."

"I have an extra blanket for you to wrap around yourself." He draped the green woolen blanket around her shoulders and patted her on one side. "There you are."

They had just finished spreading out the large blanket and

arranging the plates when Father huffed. "There are no glasses in the basket. I will just nip back and get them."

"Oh, sir, I will do it," the maid Johanna said, but Father stayed her with a hand. "We can walk back together, but I'm sure you have more than enough to do without fetching a couple of glasses for us." He waggled a finger at Diana. "Now don't eat all the pies before I come back."

Diana waved him off, then lay on the blanket, looking up at the sky. Fluffy gray clouds raced from the west, like horses at a gallop.

A few minutes later, she heard the sound of Father returning. "That was quick," she said, not getting up. But, now that she thought about it, the steps came with what sounded suspiciously like horse footfall.

Then there was a snort, a whinny and hot breath on her face.

Her eyes flew open to see a most beloved pair of warm brown eyes, attached to a most beloved horse.

She stood up, her heart pounding with joy. "Equinox!"

His mane was threaded with ribbons of every color, and he was wearing a floral wreath around his neck. Not dissimilar to the one she'd sent him down the aisle with for Fortescue all those years ago.

Hanging from the wreath was a sign. "Now what have we here?"

She looked around, but there was nobody in sight. She pulled the note off and opened it, Alec's wild handwriting leaping from the page. Her heart squeezed.

It read: *Free to a Good Home ... If You'll Have Us.*

"Who is 'us'?" Diana said to the wind. "For I am not living in a horse stall with a pony and a seventeen-hand stallion."

Templeton stepped out from behind a tree, looking glorious in a pale-blue coat and buff breeches. His long legs were encased in gleaming hessians, and his hair was its usual wild mess. "'Us' is me."

She flew to him, and he opened his arms to pull her close to him. "I got our boy back," he said into her hair. "Will you forgive me? Will you marry me?"

"Will I marry you?" she said, rolling her eyes. "You have now made it impossible for me *not* to marry you."

"That was the plan," he said.

She took the wreath off Equinox, and he wandered away to chew on the grass. "But how?" asked Diana.

Alec tucked a stray curl behind her ear, then traced his finger over it. She heard him sigh and noticed that for the first time in years, his eyes had lost their haunted look and he was completely at ease. More like the Alec of her childhood and less like the man whose world had fallen down around him. "My brilliant solicitor made Equinox the first payment back from the prince, and one he could make immediately."

"Whatever you are paying him, it is not enough. Equinox is the most perfect wedding present." Her face hurt from smiling, but she couldn't stop.

"I think so, too. Forget fine dresses, diamonds, or emeralds. There's only one wedding present for my girl."

She looked over at Equinox happily munching on grass. "A large bad-tempered stallion and the pony who makes him happy."

"Precisely."

ALL THE TRAPPINGS OF THE GOOD LIFE

It was late summer again, overcast and yet warm. The kind of still day they'd had when they'd set out on their Brighton race four years ago. The race that had changed everything.

Now, Althorne Park was home and, even though it was still a woeful old pile, building it back up was a challenge they both relished.

Had the prince paid back all the debt? No, not by a long shot. But her dowry was enough to get them started.

Diana strode across the pasture, keeping pace with Alec. "Do you think she'll ever come to like him?"

Equinox stood in one corner of the field, under a tree with Honey, while Penelope was in the opposite corner with her foal.

Alec took her hand. "He can't overcome the fact she's in charge. He's used to everyone bowing before him and Penelope refuses."

The horse bickering had been going on for so long it was a standing joke. She pushed him around, he pushed her around, and Honey just looked at them both like they were mad.

"But who do you think actually *is* in charge?"

He considered the horses, seeming to weigh his answer.

"Penelope. No doubt. She'll bring him to heel in the end. He's just too dense to catch on."

It hadn't stopped them from making three beautiful foals in their time together. "What shall we name this one?"

Alec considered it. "Well, we've got Sutton's Son and Checkers. How about 'Angel' after that pub where they drugged the grooms?"

Sutton's Son, a brown colt in his father's image, had recently won the Newmarket Stakes and put the Althorne stud on the map. Ned's son, Artie, who ran their stables, said he was as good as Equinox, although Diana secretly doubted it. No horse was as good as Equinox.

Life was everything she never thought she'd have after marriage. Instead of losing her freedoms, she'd gained them.

It had come as a surprise that she liked the challenge of being mistress of Althorne, because it was actually just making sure everything was precisely as she liked it.

Diana had a hand in running everything, from hiring staff to the household finances, and of course the stables. If she did not have much of a hand in mending and or running the kitchens, she made sure she employed people that could.

That itchy feeling of needing to escape was gone, because this life was what she needed to escape to. Making her own decisions, working by day, and loving by night. All with the man she'd adored for a lifetime by her side.

They still sparred, but instead of it ending in frustration, it ended in the bedchamber, which was highly satisfactory. She took a deep breath, loving how her heart seemed to double in size every time she thought about it.

Diana brought Alec's hand up and kissed it. "Perfect. Do you ever worry we will run out of names for their foals?"

"I don't fancy calling a horse Pease Pottage." He scrunched his nose slightly. "Maybe we could just start naming them starting with the letter *W*."

"Why *W*?"

He put his arm around her. "Because I owe my current happiness to the fact that Colonel W was a fool."

She poked him in the ribs, then softened the blow by kissing his cheek. "You owe your current happiness to having the best wife in England."

"Nothing but the truth." He turned his head and transformed the kiss into a proper one on her lips.

And there was nothing proper about it.

THE END

Thank you for reading *A Dash of Daring*. If you enjoyed this regency romance, you a might also enjoy *A Whiff of Scandal* in which Miss Daphne Davenport risks all to save her family from ruin.

Or *A Song of Secrets* in which opera singer Sarah is the very last person the vicar of Seven Oaks should fall in love with.

ALSO BY ROBYN CHALMERS

OTHER BOOKS IN THE SPIRITED SPINSTERS SERIES:
A Song of Secrets
The Lost Bride (free short story)
A Whiff of Scandal
A Moment of Mischief (2022)
A Talent for Trouble (2022)

Robyn Chalmers is an emerging author of sweet regency romance.

She lives in a country town in southern Australia with her family and a white fluffy dog. She reads a lot, walks a lot and has way too many books.

When not reading, you can find her writing her favorite kind of novel – Regency romance.

She loves hearing from readers and you can find her on Facebook, Twitter and posting bad photos of donuts on Instagram.

facebook.com/authorrobynchalmers

twitter.com/regencygal

instagram.com/robyn_chalmers_author